# Death Becomes Her

*a Gothic tale of love and...*
*body-snatching*

by Jaimey Grant

Originally written
for InD'tale Magazine
and published
June 2013 – May 2014.

# Titles by Jaimey Grant

**Connected Regencies:**

Honor
Betrayal
Deception
Intrigue
Entangled (Spellbound)
Heartless
Redemption
Forgotten, and other Heartless tales

**Short Stories, Novelettes, and Novellas:**

My Lady Coward: An Episodic Regency Romance
The 11ᵗʰ Commandment: A Serial Regency in Ten Parts
Death Becomes Her: A Gothic Regency
*The Devil She Knows* in Death Becomes Her
*Assassin's Keeper / Survival* in Unlocked: Ten "Key" Tales
*Eliza's Epiphany* in Whispered Beginnings
The Dragon's Birth (fantasy)

# Death Becomes Her

*A Regency Serial Romance by*

**Jaimey Grant**

TREASURELINE PUBLISHING

# Death Becomes Her
## A Gothic Regency

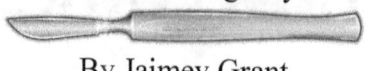

### By Jaimey Grant

*Death Becomes Her* first published in InD'tale Magazine
www.indtale.com
Compilation published by TreasureLine Publishing
www.treasurelinebooks.com
Cover designs by Laura J Miller
www.anauthorsart.com
Stock photos from
Period Images www.periodimages.com
Deposit Photos www.depositphotos.com

# Table of Contents

# Author's Note

*Death Becomes Her* was the second serial romance to appear in InD'tale Magazine. I've compiled all eleven parts here with only a few modifications from the originals.

*The Devil She Knows* was a story idea that just sort of hit me one day. Since it focuses on two of the supporting characters, I thought it would be a nice bonus for those readers who decide to download the compiled edition of *Death Becomes Her.*

It is my hope that you enjoy this compilation and the bonus story. Thank you for your continued support and encouragement.

Jainey

# Part 1:
# Sisters in Death

*England 1811*

Darkness clung to her like a lover. Melly took no notice of the lack of visibility. She lived in darkness, slumbering most of the afternoon until night's cloak fell over London. Then she would venture out with her little pony and cart, her sisters packed in the wagon with her, off to earn the money that kept them alive and off the streets.

A shovelful of dirt slid to the ground beside the hole forming before her. Her actions were swift as she removed scoop after scoop of freshly turned earth. Nothing stirred in the night, nothing disturbing the rhythmic slide of metal against dirt.

The smell of moist, warm soil wound itself around Melly's body, nearly masking the less than appealing smell that clung to her hair and skin. Refuse, decay, and rancid odors from the the River Thames assaulted her senses. Death was in the air.

Melly paused, dragging a dirt-smudged palm over her sweaty brow. Her shovel nudged something pliant, a soft object that gave a little but didn't allow the metal to slide through as the dirt did. She'd found them, finally, the latest poor souls to find their way into hell.

Doubling her efforts she uncovered the grave, signaling to her younger sisters to help her.

"Melly, I don't like it out here," fourteen-year-old Olivia whined, dutifully hunching down to get her hands under the top body, blond braid swinging as she moved.

"Patience, dear," Melly soothed, understanding her sister's reticence. Several months had passed since the last time they'd stolen bodies and Olivia had gotten used to the safety of staying out of the graveyards. "Doctor Billings pays good coin for these specimens, more if we can get them to him as soon as possible. This grave is but a few hours old so we shall receive more coin than usual."

"Do be quiet, Livy," seventeen-year-old Ashlin scolded, shoving her dark hair behind her ears as she stooped to help. "Were it not for Melly and Doctor Billings we'd all be earning our coin flat on our backs. I far prefer dead men to live ones."

The first body pulled from the mass grave thumped to the ground beside their feet. One of the older girls bent to the task of removing the clothing, tossing each piece back into the grave. They couldn't risk being transported as thieves for stealing the clothes from the bodies. Besides, the doctor didn't need clothed specimens.

Melly grimaced at her sister's summation of their situation, stooping down to lift the next body from the grave. It was true there were very few options for a poor woman, even fewer when those poor women spoke like their betters and tried to behave as them, making it plain they wanted to *be* like their betters. A few discarded primers and a determination to better herself made Melly an apt pupil who used what she'd learned to teach her younger sisters. They would not take men to their beds just to survive. They didn't have to.

Their father taught the older girls the trade, though it was unusual for women. Stealing the bodies of the forgotten, the unimportant and unloved vagrants who'd had the misfortune to die in the vast city, meant food and lodging and a little more to put by for their futures. When the schools weren't in session, they took in sewing, more to keep them in food and busy than any other reason. But sewing barely kept them fed and there was nothing left over for the future.

And Melly was determined there would be a bright future for each of them, complete with husbands and families. They'd have to change their names and move away to some small country village, find decent men who had no idea they used to earn their living as body-snatchers.

"Melly, I heard something," fifteen-year-old Belinda whispered, her gaze settling somewhere beyond them, deeper into the graveyard. She clenched her small hands in the folds of her cloak, wisps of black hair hiding her features.

"You did not," accused twenty-year-old Sadie. She straightened from her task of disrobing the dead woman at her feet, placing her hands on her generous hips in disbelief. "You're just trying to scare Livy."

"It's working," Olivia whispered, sidling closer to her oldest sister.

Melly smiled into the darkness, her sight adjusted enough in the faint moonlight to see her sisters. She was used to their complaints. As the oldest, she'd had the raising of them since Olivia's mother died birthing the child. Though only fourteen at the time, Melly had been a mother to all the girls, girls who were barely related but considered each other sisters.

"Work, girls!" Melly ordered. All five girls bent to their assigned tasks, ranging from hefting the bodies from the grave to disrobing them to tossing them into the waiting wagon that would convey them to the doctor's doorstep. One sister stood off to the side, her hands caressing an ancient blunderbuss with the confidence of one who knew the weapon well and who wasn't afraid to use it. Her twin sister held the pony and cart steady.

A collective breath released as the girls hefted the fifth and final body from the ground, freed it from its threadbare garments, and heaved it into the wagon. "Time to bury the site, girls," Melly reminded them. The sixteen-year-old twins, Ruby and Emerald, didn't move from their posts, standing as though made of stone. Olivia and Belinda climbed into the wagon to wait, taking the reins from Emerald so she could retrieve their other weapon, a rusty old dueling pistol. Stealing bodies was a dangerous business and the girls took every precaution they could within their means.

Melly, Sadie, and Ashlin each took up a shovel and

buried the grave faster than they'd uncovered it. They could not hide the fact that it had been disturbed but they'd found burying the site delayed the authorities, should the authorities choose to investigate. For mass graves filled with unloved unknowns, they often didn't.

A bridle jangled in the night. The girls froze, their shovels in mid-throw, breath coming in staccato bursts. No one moved, not even when the rider they heard passed by no more than ten feet from where they all waited.

Melly's eyes strained through the darkness, focused on the gentleman riding the black as midnight horse. Even in the faint moonlight she could tell he wore clothing of the first stare, sitting straight and tall in the saddle as if born to it. He gazed straight ahead, as if his mind was far away from his surroundings. What brought him to the graveyard at night?

He was gone moments later, his gaze never having passed their way once in his trek. Melly signaled her sisters to continue, urging them to hurry. If they lingered any longer they might not be found out by the authorities but by other resurrectionists in search of their own bodies to sell. Melly's father had told them many stories of what the body-snatchers were willing to do for an easy take. To this point, she and her sisters were most fortunate.

With the shovels tucked into the wagon and a moth-eaten blanket thrown atop the bodies, the remaining five girls piled in atop the blanket. None of them grimaced at where they sat or what they did to survive. They were long used to it.

An hour later Belinda stopped the pony before their small residence. The girls alighted, filing into the home without a backwards glance. Melly alone crawled up to the wagon seat, taking the reins from Belinda.

She offered her sister a smile, squeezing her hand over the reins. "I will return posthaste. Be sure the girls are in their beds and asleep by the time I return."

Belinda kissed her cheek. "Never worry over us, dear." Reaching down behind the seat, she grasped the pistol and laid it on the seat beside Melly. "Take care. We need you."

Melly's answering shiver had nothing to do with the chill in the air. She knew how her sisters depended on her but she also knew how resourceful they could be.

The moon hid as she guided her little pony through London's back alleys. All was dark, she noted as she neared her destination, a curious circumstance when one window should have shone with a bright light. Doctor Billings should be waiting.

Moments later she stood at the rear entrance of Doctor Billings' place of work. It was also where he taught and he lived in the rooms above. One short knock, a pause, and three more short knocks alerted the good doctor of her arrival.

It was some time before a light appeared in the window. The door swung wide, a tall figure blocking the light. It wasn't the short, rotund Doctor Billings, then, but Melly smiled all the same. "I have five good specimens for your classes, sir, various sizes and ages, two male and three female."

The man stepped out, the light spilling out from behind him. She couldn't see him well but he towered over her, at least six feet tall. He wore clothing of the first stare, indecently fitted to his muscular form. His head was bare, though she couldn't determine the exact color of his dark hair.

As dread filled her, the partial moon slid out from behind a cloud, spilling its meager light over her companion. A thunderous expression drew his heavy brows down, masking his eyes.

"What in hell are you talking about?"

Melly backed up, one step at a time, her gaze darting about. Were her worst fears about to be realized? She couldn't be captured, punished for stealing bodies from the graveyard.

His hand snaked out, fingers wrapping around her wrist and effectively preventing her flight. She cursed, a colorful word her father had taught her once long ago. Besides a slight lifting of his left eyebrow, he showed no reaction.

"Who are you and what is your business here?"

"Melly Miller," she breathed. "I deliver specimens for Doctor Billings' anatomy classes."

He cursed then, a word she hadn't heard before—and in

her world, that was something! His fingers tightened, just a touch, sending enough pain through her wrist to make her wince. He must have seen something in her movements because he cursed again and released her.

"I did not know of this arrangement," he muttered, shoving a hand through his hair. "I have need of specimens, yes, but I would rather get them by some legal, moral means." His gaze swept her from head to toe, taking in her dirtied gown and rough, woolen cloak. "Why are *you* delivering specimens?"

Melly's surprise was surely visible. She could feel her brows stretching toward her hair. "My pa made the agreement with Doc Billings and I took over when Pa died two years ago."

"You have been disturbing graves for two years?"

She didn't care for the way he said it, the hint of contempt coloring the words. She knew body-snatching was a despised activity, one many felt was the worst of offenses. Those of her own class shunned her and her sisters.

But she couldn't feel the same. The dead were nothing more than shells, left to rot. If they could serve a greater purpose, such as helping young medical students learn their craft, she couldn't think of a better use.

Drawing herself up to her full five-foot-eight-inches, she leveled him with a haughty stare. "I began doing this when I was but a girl."

"So... two years and six months?"

Interesting. The man went from contempt to amusement in less than a blink. Melly didn't care for it. Unpredictable men were dangerous. "Well over ten years have passed since I opened my first grave."

His gaze swept her form again, but she couldn't decide what he thought he'd see in the faint light. She sensed his surprise, however, and didn't wonder at it. She did not look her age. She knew that too many more years in her trade would change that. This was the last. This was the year they'd be free.

Glancing heavenward, as though looking for help or a sign of some sort, he released a pent-up breath. Stepping aside, he gestured into the kitchen behind him. "Perhaps you should come in."

Melly hesitated, swinging her head around so fast that her dark braid whipped across the man's chest. Her eyes trained on her precious pony and cart. If they lost it, there wouldn't be another any time soon. Saving for it had taken years. She didn't know this man and didn't trust him.

"What of the specimens? Where is Doc Billings? He will tell you. I need to get home to my sisters."

"Your...*sisters*?" The man rubbed a hand over his brow, as if overcome with frustration. "How did this happen?"

Melly said nothing. She strongly suspected his question was not for her. Pulling her cloak closer about her shoulders, she just waited, unsure how to hurry him along to unload the bodies and allow her to return home. It would be dawn soon and she wanted to sleep.

"I will just unload the specimens in the usual place, shall I?"

"And where is that?"

To this point, Melly hadn't really felt anything beyond a twinge of surprise at this new man answering Doctor Billings' door in the middle of the night. But now, as she received question after question and no answers to her own questions, she began to suspect all was not right. Doctor Billings had had many assistants over the years and even the occasional student who would answer the door. But never had the man answering the door not known who she was and why she was there. One or more of the gentlemen acquainted with Doctor Billings had come out to unload the bodies from her wagon to the shed near the back door.

"I will be going," she said, backing away slowly as if a swift movement might alert him to her flight and prompt him to call for help. She didn't know what she would do with the bodies in her wagon but all she worried about now was escaping possible arrest.

"No, wait. You have the bodies already?"

She nodded but didn't actually stop backing away. Her heart kicked up when he advanced, taking one step for every one of hers.

He must have realized he was frightening her. He stopped, raising both hands in a non-threatening manner. "I won't hurt you, I'm just... surprised... by all this. There was nothing in Doc Billings' papers to indicate he had an agreement with the resurrection-men."

Melly's heart sputtered, stopped, and kicked up again. Something was very, very wrong here. "Where is Doc? And who are you?"

His sigh was pulled from somewhere deep within, dragged up and out as if it had festered there for some time. "I am David Melbourne. I have taken over Doctor Billings' practice and his patients. And his school." He stared at her, then glanced up, a hint of moonlight shining brightly, for just a moment, on his upturned face.

Melly's breath caught. He was a handsome man, something she'd not had occasion to see very often. A strong jaw, firm lips, perfectly sculpted cheekbones, and even if his nose was a trifle large, he was still very pleasing to look upon. She wished she could see his eyes. What color were they?

She shook herself. This was not the time for dreaming of some strange man's eyes. He was laboring under some strong emotion, some news she was quite sure she didn't want to hear.

"Where is Doc Billings?" she repeated, her fingers tightening in her outer clothing as she tried to suppress the chill that threatened to shake her to her very core.

"He is in the anatomy room, at the moment."

She breathed out, calm suffusing her tense limbs.

"That's all right then. If you will send someone to fetch the bodies away, I can settle up with Doc and be on my way." Sending a glance toward her cart, she frowned.

Melbourne saw her concerned glance. He leaned back into the house and shouted for one of the porters. A slight man with greasy hair falling over his brow appeared and went immediately to unload the wagon. He was one Melly recognized, and though she didn't care for him, the sight calmed her further.

She smiled, the relief she felt at odds with the situation. She'd lived amongst the dead so long she'd started thinking in morbid terms. Doctor Billings was getting on in years and it was only natural that he take on an apprentice to take his place. It was curious that she'd never seen David Melbourne before but she supposed it was merely coincidence.

Melbourne opened his mouth as if to speak, swept her with an assessing look, then closed his mouth and stepped aside, gesturing for her to precede him inside. Melly bobbed a little curtsy and stepped by him, inhaling the scent of sandalwood and...death. She shivered, unsure if she imagined it or if the new doctor really did carry the smell of his trade with him.

Her eyes scanned the kitchen, seeing the spartan appearance, unsurprised. Doc Billings was very spartan himself, eschewing fashion for convenience. And what else would a doctor do? He had more important things to worry about than what he wore or how his home was decorated.

Melbourne indicated she enter a room to her left and she did so. Upon entering, she realized her fears had horrid, life-changing basis in reality.

On the table, naked as the day he was born, his middle sliced open and exposed, lay Doctor Billings.

# Part 2:
# a Deal with the Devil

**L**ittle Olivia stitched a torn hem, the firelight casting an orange glow over her hunched form. Melly stood for a moment, gazing at her bent head, wondering if now was not a better time to pull up stakes and make a new life for themselves. Her savings weren't as plentiful as she'd hoped but in light of Doctor Billings' passing, it might behoove her to consider the possibility.

"Melly." Olivia's bright blue eyes glinted in the firelight. She smiled widely at her oldest sister, but her smile faded before Melly's less than cheerful façade. "Why so glum?"

"Doc Billings is dead," Melly explained without preamble. They lived their lives moment to moment, having little time for anything other than plain speaking. She pulled her cloak off her shoulders and hung it on the peg by the door. "I don't know if the new doctor will accept the agreement we had with Doc." She didn't have the heart to tell her that not only had Melbourne *not* accepted the agreement, he'd threatened to turn her over to the magistrate for her *evil* work.

"The new doctor?"

Melly shivered and stepped closer to the meager flame in the grate. She wasn't sure if it was from the autumn chill in the air or the memory of the new doctor, but another shiver worked its way down her spine.

"David Melbourne, he calls himself. Says he's taken over Doc's school and patients."

Olivia shrugged, her eyes returning to her work. "Then he will need bodies." She glanced up, pointing at the heavy iron pot over the hearth. "There is stew, if you're hungry."

But Melly couldn't eat. Her stomach was in knots, decisions weighing heavily on her mind. With six younger sisters to care for and fret over, she had to make the best choices for all of them.

They could continue stealing the dead, delivering them to the other schools about London, but there was a greater risk in that than she cared to contemplate. Doc Billings kept them safe. He paid them more for their specimens than he paid the other resurrectionists, never telling anyone of that fact. He helped them because they let him. Melly was willing to accept it because she wanted her sisters—and herself—free from a life lived in darkness, knowing more of the newly dead than the vibrantly alive. She wanted them to have a life and families, not die as their father did, with a knife through his heart because he chose to desecrate the wrong grave.

The sigh that shook her came from so deep within that tears sprang to her eyes. This was no life for women and children. It was no life for anyone.

"Are the other girls asleep?"

"All but Belinda. She stepped out with William again."

Melly frowned. "I cannot care for that man. I think he does not see her as a wife, but rather a mistress."

Olivia shrugged, finishing her stitch and snipping the thread with her teeth. She shook out the gown she held, allowing the firelight to fall on it. Finding another rent in the soft blue fabric, she settled into stitching it up too. "Belinda is very beautiful," she said, her tone suggesting she wasn't really attending to the conversation.

"What is that to the point? It only makes her more likely to be importuned. And she is but fifteen, hardly of an age to decide anything."

"Many younger than I are already suckling their first babe, Melly," Olivia reminded her softly. "Many younger than I have already known more men than the seven of us together."

Melly's head snapped up from loosening her boot, the laces hanging limply, half undone. "What?"

Olivia shrugged. "We are poor, Melly, trash. We might none of us want to make our living on our backs but that doesn't mean we haven't tried."

Horror unlike anything Melly had ever experienced washed over her, her knees buckling. She sank into the chair beside Olivia. "You have... Belinda... all of you?"

"And you."

The girl's whisper sent shame swirling through Melly. "I admit, I foolishly did...once." Did Olivia hear the lie in the words? She gave no indication but the girl had a tendency to keep many things to herself. "I am grown and responsible for all of you. You are but a girl. How could you?"

"It was nothing, Melly. I only had to lay there while he grunted away." She shrugged in a dismissive way that brought tears to Melly's eyes. "It was nothing." Melly didn't know if her repetition was to convince herself or Melly.

"How can you say that?"

Olivia sighed, finally allowing her hands to settle in her lap. She gave her oldest sister a long-suffering look, shaking her head as if unable to believe Melly was so naïve. "We are what we are, Melly dear. We can read all the primers we want, be sure to pronounce our aitches, but it doesn't change who or what we are. We are bastards, all, and thieves of the dead. We are the worst this world has to offer." She again took up her sewing, as if she hadn't just shattered her sister's blissfully ignorant bubble.

It took Melly a moment to regain her powers of speech. When she did, she couldn't prevent a bitter tone from coloring her words. "If we are so low, why did you not continue with your new trade?"

"There is more money in body-snatching."

With that infuriatingly simple rejoinder, Melly could take no more. She shot to her feet and exited the tiny domicile. The lightening street outside offered no comfort from her raging thoughts but the cool air went far in calming the embarrassed, anxious flush heating her cheeks.

She'd failed! She'd wanted so much to save her sisters from just such a fate, save them from feeling the need to offer their bodies in order to make ends meet. That she'd sold herself once—or twice—to put food on the table when the anatomy schools were not in session, was her business and not something she was proud of. She'd done it so her sisters wouldn't have to. She'd done it because—

Who was she trying to convince? She'd done it because she was the trash Olivia said they were. She'd done it because she happened to meet someone so handsome she couldn't contain her awe, so beautiful he surely made angels weep. What rubbish!

A passing ragpicker doffed his hat to her, an odd show of respect considering who her father was. This particular man had a certain look about him that sent a pang of familiarity through Melly.

A shiver coursed her spine, and she shook off the uncomfortable feeling. Her temper had calmed so it was time to return and attempt to make some amends to her sisters, reassure them she would do what she could to make sure they needn't ever sell themselves again.

And that meant persuading Dr. David Melbourne to accept the agreement they'd had with Billings.

Olivia was already off to her bed when Melly returned. It saddened her that her sister—perhaps all her sisters were so unaffected by their decision to take men to their beds. Melly and Sadie shared the same mother, a slattern who plied her trade amongst the lesser males in existence, namely those beneath contempt but had money to spend. She returned with each of them, their father taking them in as if it was the most normal thing in the world. The other girls had similar stories, all except Olivia. Olivia's story was special.

Her feet carried her to her own bed, but a few feet from Olivia in the same small room serving as the girls' bedchamber. She'd have a few hours herself to find some rest, and then she had things to do.

The glare of the afternoon sun did little to warm the chill in the air. Melly made certain her plain black bonnet was securely tied and pulled her cloak tighter, trying to calm the nervous racing of her heart. She would see Dr. Melbourne again and this time in the light of day. She would discover just how dark his hair was and if his eyes danced when he smiled.

Her fist beat a rapid tattoo on his door, the same door she'd stood at only hours before. Her lips tipped down at her own flighty thoughts. Too much was dependent on the outcome of her meeting with him. She had no time to waste on air dreams.

Besides all that, dreaming of a man so far above her was the height of foolishness. He was a doctor, one who procured bodies from her. It would surprise her if he even thought of her as anything more than a despicable parasite earning her living off the misfortune, the grief of others.

The door flung wide, a masculine laugh climbing up her

spine. The laughter died just as soon as the doctor laid eyes on his unwelcome afternoon visitor.

"What the devil are you doing here?" he demanded. His gaze flew down the alley, first one way, then the other. Grabbing her shoulder, he dragged her into the warm kitchen, slamming the door in his wake. "Are you here to coerce more money from me? We settled up last night. I have no desire to become your latest victim."

This diatribe struck Melly dumb. Unaccountable tears sprang to her eyes but she forced them back. She'd never wept over unkindness before and she didn't mean to start now.

She also refused to contemplate the way his blue eyes flashed when he was angered.

The servants who had the misfortune of being in the room scattered. Within moments they stood alone. Melbourne gave no indication that he even noticed them. Just as Melly had always known about the elite—Melbourne's bearing declared him of the upper classes even if he was a lowly doctor now—they took little notice of the lesser beings who crossed their paths.

Unless the servants made nuisances of themselves, as Melly was doing now.

She tried to calm her temper, reminding herself that it was common amongst some of her kind to exhort more money from the doctors and anatomists who paid them for their ill-gotten gain. He had every right to be suspicious.

"I am come to inquire as to your needs," she explained with the haughty air of a duchess.

He snorted, looking her up and down in the most insulting manner. It was a look she'd grown used to. She merely drew herself up straighter, glaring down her nose at him as she awaited his response.

"You have nothing I need." His sneer was something to behold, the corner of his lip curled just so, an angry V forming above his eyes.

The hurt she felt at his tone was unlike anything she'd experienced before. Her profession elicited much disgust, even hatred. She'd learned to ignore the one and avoid the other.

Drawing on every bit of indignation she could—even while wondering if it was the wise course—she sweetly inquired, "How do you think you will teach your students if you have no bodies for them to dissect?"

"I will obtain them by some legal, *moral* means."

Melly laughed. She couldn't help it. "Legal means? You will request the bodies of murderers, those executed for their crimes? How high do you think your little school will rank, *your eminence*?" She sneered right back at him, letting her gaze slide over him the way he'd done to her. If her heart skipped a beat at the indecent way his pantaloons clung to his muscular thighs, she managed to hide it. "You may sneer at the *immoral* way I obtain specimens for your *kind*, but the ones I bring you are alone in the world. No one cares where they are or that they died."

"How do you know that?" he demanded, taking a step closer in his anger. He leaned down, shortening the distance between their faces.

Melly gazed into his harsh features, instinct telling her to step back, to flee. But she couldn't back down now. Her sisters depended on her, far more than she'd ever realized.

"I watch, or one of my sisters does. We wait sometimes, see if anyone comes to visit the grave. Other times we hear of vagrants, several tossed into one grave. These are the ones we bring to your students."

He straightened. "You mentioned sisters before. Where are they now?"

Flustered by his sudden change of subject, she faltered. "My s-sisters? They are home, still sleeping most like."

"How many?"

The way he studied her sent a tremor through her middle. Her hand went to her belly, as if to calm the upset. She could barely get a breath and she didn't even know what caused the sensation. Was it the way he cocked his head while he stared, the way his eyes narrowed as he awaited her answer? Or the way he seemed to see through her, divining the answers he sought with no response from her?

"Do you not have someone to care for you?"

Indignation flared to life. "We do not need anyone, sir! We have managed well in the years since our father died."

"And yet, here you stand before me. Begging."

Her hand tingled with the urge to slap him. "We do not beg. We never have and we never will."

He took a single step back and leaned against the large table in the center of the cozy kitchen. Crossing his arms over his chest, he asked, "Then why are you here, if not to beg me to renew the agreement you had with Billings?"

"I can see you will not discuss this matter rationally, sir. I bid you good day!" Heart sinking, she turned about to leave his infuriating presence.

"Who taught you to speak?"

The question was mild, as if satisfying his curiosity was uppermost in his mind at the moment. Really! The man's shifts in mood sent one's head spinning!

"I learned. I taught my sisters."

"Ah, yes, the elusive sisters. How many?"

Detecting no mockery in his tone, though she saw the telltale indentation of a dimple in his right cheek, she suspected he laughed at her. No matter.

Her feet took her two steps away from him, almost of their own volition. "Six. I have six younger sisters, all dependent on me and the number of bodies we can sell to the schools."

His eyes roved over her face, pausing on her mouth so long she felt the urge to fidget. Those dark blue orbs snapped up, fastening on her eyes, narrowing just a bit, as if trying to determine if she lied.

He nodded. "Then consider the agreement renewed."

Shocked, she could only stare. He smiled, the expression lighting his features in a way that reignited the heat in her middle. What was happening to her? One would think she'd never been face to face with a handsome man before!

Straightening her spine, she gave as dignified a nod as she could manage. But before she could say a word, he pushed away from the table and approached.

His smile disappeared. Standing over her, his overwhelming presence engulfed her in sandalwood and leather, something darker, something uniquely him, overshadowing it all. She inhaled deeply, almost involuntarily, a quiver starting in her belly and spreading out. Her fingers tingled but this time there was no urge to slap him. More alarming than that, she wanted to touch him, to run her fingers through his hair, determine if it was as silky as it looked.

One step back should have severed the strange trance she found herself in but her feet refused to obey her mind's desperate plea. One long finger traced a path down her cheek, the touch so gentle she almost didn't feel it. Her hands clenched, fingers laced together, memories of shared heat swirling through her brain. But that was the past, a mistake—or two, and surely the doctor wasn't so desperate for a roll in the hay that he'd proposition a body thief.

"There is a way you can care for your family," he began, his lowered voice sliding over her skin, "without desecrating graves."

Her heart sank down to her toes. She knew what he'd say before he even finished his thought, so she forestalled him the one way sure to shut him up.

She kissed him. Her lips pressed to his, tasting, tempting, teasing him into a reaction that threatened to send her to her knees. His strong arms slid around her waist, twin bands of steel pulling her as close as their layers of clothing would allow. Her body ignited, the intimate press of their bodies rekindling desires she'd thought long buried. She'd known passion, long ago, and hoped never to make that particular mistake again. But she'd reacted without thought, oddly sure the good doctor would be appalled by her actions, toss her away, refuse to ever be alone with her thus making her job easier. The opposite happened, the evidence of his desire pressing against her skirts.

Ignoring the heat, the raw desire coursing through her veins, she released his lips. Patting his cheek,  she pulled away. Her feet finally obeyed, one step, then two taking her out of range of his particular magnetism. "Thankee kindly fer the offer, love. Ye'll 'ave to work 'arder 'n that to get yer leg over me."

Melbourne took three steps back, bumping into the heavy table. He leaned back, his body slumping against the table as if he couldn't quite hold himself up. His wondering gaze slid over her again—indeed, how many times would he do that?—lingering here and there before settling back on her face.

A slow smile stretched his lips. This time, his gaze caressed her, slow sweeps that reminded her of his hands but moments ago. As he met her gaze, his dark blue eyes not nearly as dark as before, he said, "I accept your challenge."

Horror followed Melly all the way home. She threw open the door, taking no note of her sisters, her mind insisting that she had to cleanse herself of the wicked desire screaming through her. The bath awaited her, Ashlin having just climbed out, wrapping a moth-eaten linen towel about her slender, willowy form. She stepped hastily aside as Melly pushed by, the latter's clothes falling from her own slender body as she moved. She sank into the lukewarm water, a hiss of shock parting her lips.

A deluge of hot water sluiced into the tub, taking the sting of cold from her trembling limbs. The walk home, in the sudden bluster that had blown up while she was throwing herself at the doctor, should have cooled her ardor. But no. All she could think about was being back in his arms, sans clothing.

"Bah! The man is crazed, fit for Bedlam."

"Crouch? O'course 'e—*he*—is," Ruby muttered, her heavy features turning to regard Melly, brows drawn down in a menacing scowl.

Melly sat up straight in the cramped tub. "Crouch?" The resurrectionist was bad news. Flashy and charming but with an evil streak that whispered of murder rather than simple body-snatching. "What about him?"

"Blighter came 'round again," Emerald supplied helpfully, her features not so forbidding as her twin's, though no less heavy, "making threats. Heard Billings shuffled off and the new doc's refused to work with us. He wants to make sure we don't poach his lay."

Four pairs of accusing eyes settled on Melly. She'd have squirmed under their regard if she was the squirming type. Instead, she wet her hair as best she could and applied a bit of their precious soap to it, delaying the inevitable jaw-me-dead they'd heap upon her for not telling them.

A bucket of ice-cold water poured over her head, sending a wave of water out of the tub as she flew up. "Bloody 'ell!"

Sadie stood beside the tub, the empty bucket in her hand. She laughed at her sister's outrage. "Serves you right, you liar! You din't tell us Melbourne sent us packin'."

Melly shook the water and soap from her eyes. Holding out her hand for a towel, she tried to explain. "I didn't want to alarm you without reason."

Ashlin, seated at the table and preparing the week's cabbage for the cookpot, glared at her. "Without reason? Our steady income is gone and you thought that wasn't reason enough to tell us what was happening?"

Melly whipped the towel around her body, ignoring the water-soaked tendrils of hair clinging to her neck. "There is nothing to fret over," she snapped, more angry with herself than anyone. "Melbourne agreed to my terms. We will deliver more bodies as soon as may be."

The girls fell silent. Olivia piped up, her soft voice somehow managing to break through all their animosity. "They found three dead boys." She named a street only a few down from them. "They will bury them tomorrow."

"Who are they?"

Olivia shrugged. "They remain unclaimed." She frowned. "One of them appears no older than six."

"Are they burned?"

Emerald nodded. "Climbing boys."

Melly's sigh was felt by all. "Poor things."

They were all familiar with the poor, small boys forced to climb the chimneys. Often the boys perished, the heat in the chimney from recent use enough to end their pitiful lives. Parents would sell them to the sweeps, or the sweeps would find some orphaned child and take him in, replacing him with a new child when that one died. Such a shameful practice, one that tugged at Melly's maternal heart. It was something they could not change, though she'd been known to help a child or two avoid such a fate.

She moved to their shared bedchamber with Ashlin on her heels. "Will we take them to Melbourne?"

"What good do they do rotting in the ground?"

Ashlin thought about that. Then, "Perhaps none. How can we know what is right and what is wrong?"

Melly paused as she pulled a clean gown over her head, her whirling thoughts suddenly focusing on one particular thing. Settling the gown around her, she turned her back to her sister. "Will you do up the tapes?" Ashlin complied without a word, then moved to twist Melly's hair into a braid. Steeling herself, Melly asked the one question she didn't want to. "Do you, or any of the girls, take men to your beds?"

Ashlin's fingers stilled in Melly's hair. "Why do you ask?"

Lungs deflating, Melly closed her eyes, wishing she'd been able to do better for her sisters. "I am so sorry, Ash," she whispered. "I swore I'd remove you all from this, let you have husbands and families."

Gentle fingers cupped her cheeks. Her eyes opened, meeting her sister's pale blue eyes. "Melly dear, what we have done is not your fault. We made choices, each of us, and each of us decided it was not the best." Her hands dropped, one slim shoulder lifting in a shrug. "It may not have been the best decision but it was mine. I've had very few decisions of my own."

"Is that what you want," Melly demanded, hands on hips, "to make your own decisions?"

"Oh stubble it, Melly," Sadie ordered as she strode into

the small room. "You pretend as though we cannot take care of ourselves. Whatever made you think you are our mother?"

"I..." She paused, choking back tears, steeling her resolve. "I am the only mother any of you have ever known!"

Ashlin took her hands, squeezing gently. "And we adore you for that, Melly, truly we do. But if we want to survive in a way other than stealing bodies, in a way less damning, should we not be allowed to try?"

"But—"

"But nothing!" Sadie snapped. "Our lives, Melly. Ours! You put on these 'igh and mighty airs, make us do the same. We are rubbish! We will never marry, unless there is a man desperate for a proper family. We are dirt, Melly, dirt!"

Unable to respond, Melly stared, her eyes swimming with tears. Her mind could barely comprehend what she was hearing. She'd only ever wanted the best for her sisters, the most important people in her life.

Bah! Perhaps she was better off leaving them all behind and taking the doctor up on his implied offer.

Horrified that she could even think such a thing, Melly straightened her spine. "What you choose is up to you, certainly. I will not prevent you."

Air, her lungs screamed. Air. All she needed, again, was air. A moment to breathe, to ponder all that she'd discovered and experienced in such a short time. She pulled on her boots without bothering to lace them up, caring little of the danger of tripping posed by such a careless action.

The air without did nothing for her, the cold combined with her wet hair sending a shaft of pain through her head. Her lungs burned, each labored breath threatening to send her into oblivion. She fought for calm, fought for the collectedness that kept her sane through the nightmares.

All her energy, for years, had been taken up with bettering their lot in life, saving up for the moment when they could say goodbye to London's East End, and make lives for themselves in some quaint village. One single time nearly a year ago she'd been offered enough money to sell herself, one payment that gave them nearly enough to quit everything. To this day, she didn't know what it was about her that tempted that gentleman to spend so much for a tumble, but she wasn't too proud to accept it. With that generous offering, they needed but one more season of body-snatching to see the final end of their detestable lives. Finally.

She stopped, in the overcast street, her eyes seeing nothing of the people around, her body feeling nothing of the sharp breeze. Her sisters didn't need her anymore, refused to accept her care. What was the point in saving for a future her sisters didn't want?

What was she to do now?

# Part 3:
# Death holds no Surprises

Six girls gaped at the bounty laid before them. Flimsy banknotes, shiny guineas, and numerous smaller coins taunted them with the bright things they could buy.

Nothing could have surprised them more than the moment Melly had strode into the hovel, snatched up an ugly, slender-topped vase from a shelf by the fire, and smashed the thing open on the large table. The contents had been far more than any had guessed. Even Melly stared in awe, not having realized how such savings would look when piled just so.

"What—! Where did you get all this?" Ruby asked, her round, heavy features more shocked than Melly could ever recall.

"I tol' ye I been savin' fer our future. What in 'ell did ye think that meant?" she snapped, still so angry and disheartened to even keep to her usually refined speech. She breathed deep, crossing her arms over her chest and squeezing tight, hugging herself against the chill in her veins. "This is the last season of body-snatching. I have enough to start over, rent a small cottage in some village where we are not known, put ourselves out there to catch husbands. One more season." Her exhale was a long sigh from her deepest self. "But some you have expressed the desire to make your own decisions. I have decided to divide the money, let you all choose the paths your lives take from here."

Six stunned gazes fixed on her. She met none of their

shock, staring instead on the single £50 note laying just under a pile of pennies. With little conscious thought, she touched it, her thoughts caught up in laughing blue eyes and guinea gold locks, remembered delight, mutual desire, and a sense of completion. Feeling barely a twinge of remorse for her actions now—unlike her actions then—she took it, ignoring the gasps from her sisters.

"I earned this," she explained, "and I don't expect any of you to share what you've earned in the same manner." Was the ice coating the words enough to portray her disappointment in all of them, herself included?

Ashlin's voice broke through her memories. "How many men did you pleasure to earn that?" Her tone held no judgment, just a plethora of curiosity.

"One," Melly whispered, barely believing her own claim. It was unheard of, impossible to earn so much from one encounter. More so when one hadn't expected payment in the first place.

Sadie laughed, long and loud. "You 'spect us to believe you earned fifty quid from one tumble?"

"I don't expect you to believe anything," Melly sighed. "But it is true, so I will take this as my portion. Divide the rest how you see fit."

She'd never attempted to retrieve bodies alone but that's

exactly what Melly found herself doing the following night. She didn't know what her sisters were doing and tried not to think about it. Olivia had claimed they didn't care to continue whoring but when none of them joined her as she readied the pony and cart, she realized she didn't know what to expect from them anymore. With a heavy heart, she'd left to tend to their dark business alone.

The boys Olivia had mentioned, the poor little climbing boys who'd died performing their detestable chimney climbing duties, lay one on top of the other in an unmarked grave. Melly had to continue working, even if her sisters refused to, because her fifty quid would not support her for long. So she applied shovel to dirt, scoop after scoop, until the tool struck against something soft.

Moments later, she was stripping three young lads of their meager covering and settling them into the wagon bed. Her mind shied away from the loneliness of retrieving three boys while her sisters did whatever is was they'd decided to do. A single tear slipped down her cheek, a tear for the poor dead boys and the loss of the dream she'd held so close.

Shaking off such maudlin sentiments, she settled the bodies in the cart and threw a blanket over them. As she climbed into the seat, unease skittered over her flesh, so intense that she found herself glancing about her as if expecting some creature to leap upon her from the inky shadows. Reaching behind her, she grasped the ancient pistol and placed it in her lap, then she clicked her tongue at the pony and started off to Melbourne's.

The porter showed Melly into the dissecting room. As she turned to question his actions, the man disappeared to retrieve the bodies from her cart. Turning back, she beheld Melbourne at the table, elbows deep in a body. Her eyes drifted about the room, not caring to see the end result of her own business.

Candles burned on every available surface, washing the room in a golden glow. Large windows on two walls would provide light during the day but now, in the blackest part of the night, the curtains blocked any moonlight that might have managed to infiltrate the room.

He was an odd doctor, plying his trade in the wee hours, and meeting her face to face instead of relying on a hospital porter or his surgical assistant to negotiate trade between them. She'd yet to determine exactly what to make of the man. He treated her with the utmost contempt one moment, then regarded her with undisguised hunger, as if he'd devour her whole given half the chance. He was a baffling contradiction; one she was quite sure she should avoid.

With that thought firmly in mind, she forced her eyes to continue sweeping the room, determinedly ignoring the man who was at that moment stretching the entrails of his subject on the table beside him. On one wall was a massive painting depicting the dissection of a man. Men stood all around the body, one man clearly teaching the others. An anatomy class? Melly could barely look at the painting without shuddering, musing that much the same thing was happening no more than a few steps behind her.

"Miss Miller."

The deep murmur sent heat through her middle. She turned, beholding the doctor wiping his long-fingered hands on a large cloth. Struck anew by his handsomeness, she stared, her eyes sweeping over his high cheekbones and shadow-darkened eyes. A smile played about his firm lips, lips she recalled pressed to hers just days before. The heat in her middle spread to the rest of her body.

Her gaze swept down, over his linen and apron-clad chest, settling on his bare arms. Blood smeared his muscular forearms, his sleeves rolled back to the elbows to prevent soiling his shirt. Though he'd failed in that, she noted, seeing the red smudge near his shoulder. This tiny mark that marred his perfect, masculine appearance allowed her to gather her composure about her like a cloak.

"I did not mean to intrude. The porter showed me in here."

The towel in the doctor's hands, a macabre spectacle of red and white in the dancing candlelight, was tossed into a basket in the corner. "I told him to," Melbourne replied, untying the apron from about his waist and slipping the thing over his head. It followed the towel into the basket. He began unrolling his sleeves. "I wanted to see you."

Not "speak with you" or "discuss the terms of our agreement." Warning bells sounded in Melly's mind, urging her to flee. Determined to prove she could withstand this man's abuse, she straightened her spine and managed to look down her nose at him.

"What makes you think you have any claim on my time?"

He smiled, just the slightest quirking of his lips. "I think your challenge gives me that right."

Her jaw dropped. Challenge? His silly little belief that she'd somehow challenged him to seduce her?

"That *challenge* is meaningless, sir, the product of your fertile mind." She drew herself up straighter, though she had no more height at her disposal. Drawing her worn cloak closer about her shoulders, she added, "I am not interested in a quick tumble from a doctor who finds pleasure in making me feel like a common criminal."

"You are a criminal," he stated unequivocally, "though I would call you uncommon. I'd never heard of a female involved in the ugliness you enjoy until I saw you on my doorstep."

Rage swelled in Melly's breast. She marched up to him, heedless of the bloody misery on the table beside him. Stabbing a finger into his chest—and nearly distracting herself with the observation that he was solid muscle under his linen shirt—she snapped, "I do not enjoy my work, you puffed up peacock! I do this because I see the greater good that can be done by dissecting these poor souls. I do this to earn money so I can save my sisters from this darkness."

Her voice shuddered on the last few words, her mind sliding inexorably to the very girls who caused much of her recent upset. She could not let their betrayal control her own thoughts and actions. They were right in that they deserved to choose their own paths in life, but she did not have to like the choices they made. And she did not understand how any of them could choose selling their own bodies over selling dead ones, even if other people viewed their theft as the lowest act a being could commit.

Biting her lip against her own emotions, she stated much more calmly, "I do not care for your insults and your contempt. If I were a man—"

"If you were a man, I wouldn't be able to do this."

He jerked her into his arms before the final word had left his mouth. Melly had little time to react, but in the last possible thread of time, she did, her knee coming up with unerring accuracy. It was a trick her father had taught her and Sadie and one they'd taught the rest of their sisters. It was small protection and might not save them from a savage beating, but it was better than nothing.

Melbourne hit his knees with a bone-jarring crunch, his hands protectively cupping his nether regions. Melly leapt back, her chest heaving with the force of her upset. A momentary pang of regret, a twinge of guilt, shot through her at her actions but she shook it off. The man touched her without her consent, and he deserved what he got.

Before he could recover, Melly fled the premises.

David groaned, squeezing his eyes so tight stars blossomed. How could he not have considered the girl might defend herself? Perhaps the fact that she kissed him the last time. Hell. What a fool he was.

A low chuckle sent his eyelids flying up. A masculine face came into slow focus, blond curls and an all too familiar expression adding extra humiliation to David's situation. Fighting the urge to groan again, he glared at the younger man crouching before him.

"Leave off, James," he muttered.

James offered him a hand. David rose, gingerly, trying to ignore the dull throbbing that seemed to radiate from his groin to all his extremities.

"Bit of a to do, brother?" James asked, his grin widening. "Who was the pretty creature who felt the need to unman you?"

David scowled. "Nobody of interest to you, whelp."

James' laughter filled the candlelit chamber. "But she seems delightful, bringing you to your knees."

David struck out, smacking his younger sibling on the

shoulder. "She is a hellion, a miserable thief."

"What did you do to her?" James attempted to school his features into something resembling a serious mien, but his lips twitched suspiciously.

David turned his back on his brother, focusing instead on the body on his table. "Tried to kiss her, if you must know."

James stepped back, his gaze sliding over the room and settling on the door through which the girl had just fled, his mind churning with the implications of what just occurred. "Why?"

Casting a questioning glance over his shoulder, David asked, "Why what?"

"Why did you want to kiss her? Is she not the girl who delivers the bodies for your students?"

The contempt in James' voice sent a swirl of unaccountable anger through David's chest. Unsure where that feeling came from or why, he simply nodded, unwilling to discuss the matter more. He set about cleaning up the mess on his table instead.

James dropped the subject, instead offering his brother a hand cleaning up what, to him, was a normal sight in the small domicile. He'd spent time at the doctor's school, not to learn, but to annoy his brother. David tolerated his presence, as did the late Doctor Billings, but James often came with requests for money. David's funds were modest, enough to fund his brother's mad starts, but lately the younger man asked for more and more, far beyond what David could spare.

"How much do you need?" he asked, an internal sigh never reaching his lips. He stuffed the intestines of his specimen back into the body cavity, annoyed that he still didn't know what killed the man. It was curious. He was young, not yet twenty, had no outward signs of trauma, no symptoms of poisoning, nothing to explain why he ended up dead. David enjoyed medical mysteries but only when he solved them.

The silence lengthened. David turned, his eyes settling on his younger brother. Dread crawled its way into his throat. "How bad is it?"

James shrugged, his ready smile strained at the edges. "Not bad," he hedged, "a monkey...or ten."

David's heart stuttered. "You need £5000? How could you let that happen?" Anger replaced dread. "Of all the irresponsible, pigheaded, stupid things to do, James! £5000?" He slammed his fist on the table, the body jumping as if startled. "How do you expect me to settle that kind of debt?"

James shrugged.

The other man's response was unsatisfactory to an older brother who'd spent many years rescuing him from his own thoughtless actions. David shoved away from the table, his hand slamming into James' chest. The force of the blow sent James stumbling back, his lanky form falling into the chair against the wall.

"When will you grow up, James? I can't rescue you anymore."

"Why not?"

"I don't have £5000!"

James' look of shock was something to behold but David was too busy fighting down the humiliation of having to inform his brother of his lack of funds to really notice. "I have a mere £100 to my name, James. The rest is gone."

"On what? You never spend a groat."

"Except on you, dear brother." David sighed, slumping into the chair beside James. "The last £500 you asked for was the last I could spare. I have bills here, instruments to buy, cadavers, equipment. I need to keep this school afloat and to do that, I need to stop funding you."

James said nothing, his face, for once, wiped clean of all amusement. "That's that, then, isn't it?" he mused. He glanced down at his hands. "I will leave you, then, and search for a solution on my own."

David had nothing to say. He wanted to help but could see no way to do so. So he stared at the body on the table, again, allowing his mind to ponder that mystery instead of the question of his brother's finances.

James stood, opened his mouth, and then snapped it shut.

A whirlwind burst into the chamber. Melly Miller.

David shot to his feet as a breathless Melly stammered incoherently in his direction. Just as he opened his mouth to ask her to repeat herself, the porter entered with the body of a girl clutched to his chest.

David moved to Melly's side while James cleared the table behind them so the porter could deposit his burden there. Melly's eyes were glued to the scene, the once gruesome sight of blood and gore now replaced with a pretty blond girl, horribly beaten, pale blue dress torn and bloodstained, the shallow movement of her chest attesting to her fragile grip on life.

Remembering the last time Melly stood before him, David refrained from touching her, though he wanted to soothe the upset tensing her slim form. "Who is that?"

"Olivia," Melly breathed. "She's been attacked. I found her. Help her. Please!"

There was so much emotion in her words, so much pain and fear that David jumped to the only logical conclusion. "Your sister?"

The slightest hesitation occurred, a breathless moment in time, almost imperceptible. She shook her head. "My daughter."

# Part 4:
# Death changes Nothing

Olivia didn't survive the night. Melly sat in a chair by the wall, her mind blank, her body numb. She didn't know what to feel at the moment, didn't know how to go on without the bright, quiet girl. Olivia's presence had been one of calm, patience, and sense when chaos threatened to dominate. Without her, Melly wasn't sure what to do.

The world thought she was her sister, the age of the girl fitting rather nicely with the ages of the other girls. No one thought much of Melly's father taking in another stray. He'd gained the reputation of doing such long before. And Melly'd hidden her pregnancy well. Sadie was the only one who knew the truth—at least as far as Melly knew.

So Melly had been a mother and sister to Olivia. She was sure the girl never knew and part of her regretted that. But she never thought she could tell her, never wanted to admit to her ignorant mistake all those years ago. Melly hadn't wanted anyone to know she'd followed in her own slattern mother's footsteps and given herself to a man in exchange for money.

And now, poor Olivia was gone, all of Melly's sisters had made the same foolish mistake Melly had, and—

She sat up straight. All her sisters had made the same mistake. How many of them would end up pregnant? And more frightening, would they seek out an abortionist like so many in the same situation did, dying in their quest to rid themselves of the child?

David walked into the room, his gaze settling on Melly's

still form. She stared at the body on the table, but David suspected she wasn't really looking at the girl. Her eyes held fear and grief, as her every emotion was drawn inward. It was the closest he'd seen Melly come to breaking.

"Miss Miller?"

"Melly," she muttered almost too low to hear. "You says Miss Miller and I don't know who yer talkin' to." Her modulated tones slipped, but she didn't seem to care.

The urge to wrap his arms around her, soothe her upset, rose to taunt him. He was too aware of the distance between them, however, more than just the natural distance of their places in Society. Melly herself had established rather eloquently that she desired him to keep his distance, the memory of her method causing him to wince, considering it was but yesterday when she made her point.

"Melly," he conceded, aware that she barely attended him at any rate, "things must be arranged. Would you consider leaving her to me?"

Melly's gaze lifted, meeting his. "What?"

The horror in her eyes struck him in the chest. He didn't understand. She'd said she believed more could be learned from dissecting a body than leaving it to rot in the ground, yet her reaction indicated she shared the same feeling as many others, that dissection was part of the punishment doled out to murderers.

His tongue tied, he just stood there.

She rose, slowly, every movement of her body exaggerated with the force of her rage, as if she put every effort into not rending him limb from limb. Her steps carried her across the room until she stood just before him.

"You stood there, as did I," she fumed, her harsh whisper seeming loud in the enclosed space. "You heard what she said, her final request."

He had. He'd not wanted to hear it, however, in the final moments of the young girl's life. He'd not wanted to believe he couldn't save her, that the years of anatomy lessons and learning the human body was all for naught. He'd been unable to save her and that galled him. The look in Melly's eyes had been so hopeful, so trusting that he'd doubled his efforts, praying to any higher power who would listen that he could save the child's life.

His failure put the despair in Melly's eyes, but his request returned the flame of anger, the outrage of a mother insulted, nay, tormented after losing a child.

Yet, there was so much more to learn. He couldn't, in good conscience, allow a specimen to go into a grave, left there to rot and do nothing for humanity, no matter how heartless it sounded in the moment.

"She asked that you not dissect her. However desperately you desire it, whatever my beliefs, I will honor her request, the request of a girl who had everything taken from her. Everything!"

Put that way, David could do nothing but agree, despite

the very real disappointment he felt at such a waste.

Melly glanced from Olivia to David. "Can I trust you to ready her for burial?"

Despite her justified reason for such a question, anger flared in David's chest. He tamped it down. "Yes, Miss Miller, you can." James reentered the room but Melly and David ignored him. "I'll even pay for those fancy bars to keep others of your ilk from stealing her body."

Melly scowled at him, making her way out of the room. As she passed James, she stopped, her dark brows shooting upward. "What are you doing here?" Her gaze darted behind him, as if expecting someone else to be lurking out of sight.

David's frown was reflected in his explanation. "My brother James was here throughout. You must not have noticed him before."

Her brow furrowed, but she said nothing as she slipped from the room.

"How will you afford those fancy bars, brother?" James murmured, his gaze locked on the closed door. He glanced at David. "They do not run cheap."

David ignored him. "What did she mean?"

James' expression went from mildly inquiring to suspiciously blank. "Just what you said. She didn't notice me before."

"You're hiding something."

"You should learn to trust a body, Davey," James

retorted, smiling at the reaction he got. He dodged to the right, narrowly missing the chair by the wall. David followed, grabbing his brother by the shirtfront.

James held up both hands. "Do not mar my pretty face! I concede, I am hiding something, but nothing of any import."

David released him. "Then what?"

"Her face seems familiar. Are you sure she's the same body-snatcher Billings used?"

"Positive."

"Hmm. Then perhaps I am mistaken."

James made to leave but David wouldn't let him. "Explain that."

"She reminds me of a little whore I met last year, that's all. As I said, nothing of import."

Her sisters sat around the table, preparing the soup pot for the next week's worth of sustenance. Melly silently hung her cloak up on the hook by the door. Closing her eyes, she allowed just a moment for the desolation to sweep over her, one moment of weakness before telling her sisters where she'd been for the last several hours.

Only hours—not lifetimes—had passed since Melly had left the doctor's, her goal to return home to her sisters and convince them once and for all that though body-snatching was surely the lowest form of profession, it was certainly more desirable than whoring. Granted, they'd not sounded much like they were going to go down that road but with two headstrong misses like Sadie and Belinda, one never knew.

She'd never made it home. Only one street over from the doctor's she'd found Olivia, bloodied and exposed, the victim of a cruel attack. Her heart had been in her throat ever since.

Melly didn't know now how she'd managed to get the girl back to Melbourne's. Every passing second, the girl's breath growing fainter and fainter, had sent panic spiraling through Melly's heart. One thought spun in her mind, one unshakable belief.

Melbourne could save her.

Shaken, weary, and spiraling into the depths of a melancholy she'd never anticipated despite her morbid profession, Melly pushed away from the wall to encounter five pairs of inquiring eyes.

Daylight had risen, the girls were up with the dawn, and Melly had an overwhelming urge to lay down on her bed and sleep for the next several months. Life wasn't fair, a lesson her father taught her long before the world did. But losing Olivia was so much more than simple unfairness. It was a stark reminder that life was fragile, precious, and they played a dangerous game.

"Did Olivia find you?" Ashlin asked, her eyes sliding

back to the carrot she chopped. "She decided to help you and departed before we could join her."

Sadie snorted, crouching down to stir up the coals under the soup pot. "As if you needed any of us, Melly. You can do it all on your own, can you not?" Her exaggerated tones mocked Melly as surely as they mocked the upper classes they aped.

Rage, black and red, without direction or purpose, suffused Melly's exhausted limbs. Her fingers clenched at her sides. She wanted to throttle her sisters for allowing Olivia to leave alone. It was as if they had no concept of the danger out there, the danger that threatened them every second of every day.

It would do no good. She forced calm, forced her fingers apart, prayed for a bit of strength and clarity to get through the next months. Olivia had known the dangers when she'd ventured out alone, just as Melly had. They'd still done it, with grave results. They all knew the dangers they faced, were reminded almost daily by the presence of other, dangerous resurrectionists, ones who would kill for the money the body would bring. Olivia knew.

Melly's eyes filled with tears, grief overtaking the rage. "No, Olivia didn't find me," she choked out, sucking in a breath in an attempt at calm, "but I found her."

Olivia was duly laid to rest. Her sisters—David wasn't sure he'd ever think of them as anything else—stood around, eerily silent, tears streaming down their young faces. Melly, however, remained impassively beautiful, back straight, face clear, arms around two of her sisters. She held herself so stiffly that though it appeared she was holding up her sisters, he suspected the opposite was true. David got the impression that if they let go, she'd shatter.

How much did they know of Olivia's parentage? Did Melly even know the girl's sire?

And on that thought, he shut down, unwilling to entertain the anger that coursed through him at the thought of her with another man. With his brother. She'd borne a child when no more than a child herself. The possibility that she was indeed the same woman his brother remembered was strong. David wasn't sure what to do if it was true. Or that there was anything to do. What had any of it to do with him?

Survival depended on the bodies Melly and her sisters could sell. So the night following Olivia's burial, her sisters again joined her in the graveyard under the complete darkness of a moonless night, shivering together as the mist coated them from head to toe.

The acquisition of three men, two women, and a child

was a boon that Melly hadn't anticipated. One grave, the week's recent dead poor tossed in with no care, refuse to be disposed of rather than loved ones to be mourned.

The thought threatened to send Melly into a fit of weeping, but she restrained the impulse and did what had to be done. The bodies were placed in the wagon, six silent women attending to each of their assigned duties while the midnight mist soaked through their thin cloaks and into their bones.

Melly dropped her sisters at home, watched them file silently in, then turned the pony toward Melbourne's. She didn't want to see the doctor, not after he'd kept his word and fitted Olivia's grave with the fancy steel bars designed to keep "her kind" out. It was an expense she could never have afforded, one that surely must have been difficult even for Melbourne. She owed him and she hated that.

Melly sneezed. The mist would surely make her ill, but again, there was little help for it. She had to work, at least until the days grew long and they could finally leave this life behind them.

Her fist beat a rapid tattoo on the door. She assumed the porter would be the only person she'd have to deal with this night, as midnight was long gone and the doctor would surely not be out of his bed. She'd seen him awake during the day and the middle of the night, though, so she was starting to think he never slept.

The porter, yawning and scratching at his chest, greeted

her with a surly nod. She forced a smile, and pointed to the wagon behind her.

"I've a delivery. I'll just leave 'em in the shed, shall I?"

The porter shrugged, yawned again, and shut the door in her face.

Melly's eyes widened at his rudeness, but she turned about. It wasn't the first time she'd had to unload the bodies herself, and it probably wouldn't be the last. The quicker she had it done, the quicker she could return home and sleep.

Not allowing her mind to focus on any one thing, Melly set to work, pulling the bodies from the cart and dragging them to the small shed where Melbourne kept them until he needed them. Once she had all the bodies piled before her, she opened the door.

The smell threatened to send her backward, but she steeled her spine and tossed the smallest body in. She managed to hoist the female bodies over her shoulder, hobble in, and toss them down. The men, however, she had to drag and push. By the time she'd gotten two of the three in, she was sweating in the damp chill, her lungs heaving in her chest.

A sound came from behind her, nothing to make her stop her work but enough that her mind registered the odd, shuffling noise. Probably a dog or some such, foraging. It was as she closed the shed, wiping her hands on her cloak, that she realized the sound wasn't a dog at all.

She opened her mouth, but no sound emerged. Pain blossomed in her chest, but she couldn't tell why. Her mind fogged over, disallowing a single coherent thought to remain. The wet street rose to meet her face.

As she fell, she heard a voice, laughter, as if from a great distance.

"Another body for the doc."

# Part 5:
# Death changes Everything

**D**avid Melbourne was a quiet, peaceful man, not prone to outbursts of emotion. Since meeting Melly Miller, he doubted he knew himself at all. She had him twisted in knots, sending him into confusion one moment and anger the next. And then she'd have him laughing, and then mourning right along with her.

Now, he felt fear unlike any he'd ever known. He clutched Melly's limp form to his chest, dawn shedding its cold gray light over them as he hurried through the rear entrance of the anatomy school. How many more of these Miller girls would he have on his table? It wasn't right, though he knew some would disagree with him on that particular point. Body-snatchers were the devil's workers, filled with greed and no respect for the dead. What better place for them to end up than right where they placed so many others?

David, though needing their services, had long considered them in much the same light. But he'd gotten to know Melly, little by little, each verbal battle they fought revealing more about her than she realized. Through her, he'd come to know a little of her sisters as well. They were young women, alone but for each other, doing what they must to survive.

Some might have declared there was less damnation in selling themselves, but the mere thought of Melly doing such a thing filled him with an anger he didn't understand. Surely it was her life and her decision to make? What possessed him to think one choice in her life was better or worse than another?

None of that mattered at the moment. Before he could indulge in wondering at his odd, possessive emotions, he had to save her life. The blood covering her upper body filled him with unease. He couldn't tell from a simple glance just where it was coming from or what caused it.

Of all the nights for him to sleep like an ordinary human being! He didn't even know she would deliver bodies so soon after her sister's—daughter's passing. Had he known he might have waited up, met her himself, if only to tell her that she should show some respect, grieve properly.

None of that mattered now. He had to save her and he could only pray he would succeed.

As gently as he could, he placed her upon the very same table he'd used for Olivia. He tried not to think of the other girl, refused to remember the pleading look on Melly's face as he'd operated on the pale, younger version of herself.

No one stood by pleading with him now. It was just him and her.

Stripping her of her cloak and tossing it aside, he gently cut away her bodice. Blood coated her pale flesh, so much that he couldn't immediately tell where it started. Much of it had dried, making the coarse fabric of her gown adhere to her skin. But as his fingers probed her flesh, he found the source. Near her side, just under her left breast, he noticed the gash, a puncture wound he recognized all too well.

Cursing under his breath, he left her side for a moment,

just long enough to call for Dobson, the porter. Returning to her side, he did what he could while he waited for the man to come with fresh water and rags. Her injury was serious, though he was hopeful since she still lived. The other victims of this sort of stabbing had been delivered to him already dead, the knife having slid between ribs and entering the heart. Melly was fortunate, very fortunate indeed. The knife just missed her heart. She'd have a long, painful recovery, but she would recover.

If infection didn't set in.

The porter returned, water, rags, and freshly boiled instruments.

"Find candles," David ordered, "as many as you can. Open the drapes to let in what little daylight there is. I need to see!"

The porter did as bid, the room flooding with light. David breathed a short-lived sigh of relief.

When the man came close, he smirked, "Got a live one again, eh, Doc?" His gaze settled on the figure on the table.

David shot a frown over his shoulder, but turned his head fully when he saw the look on the other man's face. "What ails you, man?"

"That's—that's—"

"Miss Miller. I found her by the cadaver shed." David promptly returned his full attention to properly cleaning the wound in preparation of stitching it closed. He had no time for his porter's megrims.

"She was here. Mere hours since."

"William Dobson, I don't have time for your reminisces!" David snapped, though he did note the man's words enough to realize Melly might have been out there for hours in the cold, dirty street. "The bleeding has stopped, but her breathing is shallow. I have to stave off infection and it might already be too late for that."

He ignored Dobson, barely noting when the man sidled from the room, his mind going over every possible thing that could go wrong as he examined the wound for possible internal damage, relieved to find her assailant had been far more inept than he had been with previous victims. Satisfied that she'd heal properly, he slid the needle in and out, drawing the torn flesh back together.

Infection was his biggest worry. She'd lain in a dirty alley for hours before he'd happened upon her, on his way to the shed to see if there were any bodies left in there that needed brought in. He hadn't known she'd been there, delivering more when she should have been in mourning for her sister—daughter.

A banshee wail rent the early morning silence. Melly's body jerked, the needle slipping from David's fingers. He stumbled back, more shocked than he cared to admit. Stupid! He'd become so used to the bodies on his table being incapable of movement that he hadn't considered Melly would wake.

Shaking off his surprise, he returned to her side, placing

a gentle hand on her arm. She thrashed away, nearly throwing herself from the table in her agitation. "Melly," he soothed, "be easy. You've been injured and I must stitch the wound. Let me finish."

Tears sprang to her eyes. Lips trembling, she choked out, "Wha—how—?" Her fingers fluttered, arm rising off the table. She tried to raise her head but gasped out, tears escaping to streak her cheeks.

David settled a hand on her forehead, gently massaging, his other hand sliding up and down her arm. Though he needed to finish stitching her up, he couldn't have her causing more damage than she'd already suffered either. She must calm herself.

She whimpered, tears flowing freely. Her hands flexed, as if seeking purchase in something, anything to relieve the pain and tension in her body.

He took her hand, keeping his other on her brow. Her grip was much stronger than he'd expected under the circumstances, and he took heart from this one small thing.

"Melly, let me help you."

Panic slid over her dirt-smudged features. Her whimpers increased, shaking her upper body in a way that made him realize that in his hurry to help her, he'd neglected to afford her a shred a dignity. Granted, her wound was in such a place that he could only partially cover her. Still...

He reached for a nearby rag, swiftly draping it over her. Fresh blood seeped from the half-stitched wound, sending bright rivulets down her side. If she didn't calm, and soon, she'd bleed to death on his table. He could dose her with laudanum but he wasn't sure she was lucid enough at the moment to take it without choking.

"Livy..."

He didn't hear that. He couldn't. He wouldn't think of Olivia Miller and and the fact that he'd lost her not more than a sennight past on this very table. He wouldn't consider the very real possibility that he could lose Melly as well.

He cursed himself. Such musings would help no one. Leaning close, he whispered, "You are safe now, Melly. Safe here with me. I will help. But you must still your limbs so I can see what I need to do to help you."

Her eyes focused on him, pain clouding the dark blue, tears glistening on her lashes. Her fingers clenched on his, lips firming against the pain. Her eyelids slid shut and she managed the slightest nod of her head. Every muscle in her body remained tense, but she stilled, just as he asked.

"Good girl," he murmured, deeply impressed. Then, in a move he barely understood, he leaned forward, pressing his lips to her forehead. Her body eased on the table. David stared at her, relief flooding him. She'd fainted.

Unwilling to make her go through the horror of waking on the table again, he made swift work of cleaning the gash once more, stitching her up, and covering the wound with clean cloths. He'd have to change the bandage often to help stave off infection.

Winding a long strip of clean linen around her middle, across her breasts, he pondered his next action. He did not care for the idea of returning her to whatever hovel she shared with her sisters. Other than their no doubt loving care, what else could they do for her? He very much doubted they had the means necessary to care for a wound like hers, make sure she had proper nourishment and rest. Hell, he doubted they'd be able to keep her in her bed long enough to heal! She'd return to her trade before her sisters could blink.

There was no help for it, he decided, ignoring the odd thrill that went through him at the thought. She'd have to stay with him.

# Part 6:
# Recovering from Death

Seeing Melly settled comfortably in his own bedchamber, David went in search of Dobson. The porter had said something that nagged at David, something important.

He found Dobson in the kitchen, shoveling eggs into his mouth faster than the little cook could put them on the plate. David marched across the small room to yank the porter from his seat. The chair clattered backward, startling the cook.

David ignored all this, pushing his face up to Dobson's. "Explain your earlier words."

Dobson's eyes went wide, fear and shock flickering through his watery green eyes. "What words?"

"In regard to Miss Miller. You said you saw her hours ago, at the shed. What did you mean?"

"Delivering bodies, she were!" Dobson sputtered. "Like usual, sir."

"Why did you not put them in the shed, Dobson?" David snarled, rage sliding up his throat with every word Dobson uttered. "Why was she out there alone?"

Dobson sputtered something incomprehensible. The cook grabbed David's arm. "Sir! You'll kill 'im, you will!"

The cook's nasal whine broke through David's anger. He barely recognized himself in the vengeful man he now displayed, but there was no help for it. "Gah!" He released Dobson, the man stumbling away with a hand to his throat. "You allowed a woman to unload dead bodies...alone... in the middle of the night?"

"Dug 'em up, din't she? She can toss 'em in the shed. Bloody ghoul."

David lunged at Dobson, but the cook held tight, unwilling to let him kill the porter as he so rightly deserved. David could have thrown the wiry cook across the room but he'd starve without the little man. Enough sense had returned to prevent that catastrophic action.

Dobson stood back, his features as shocked as a man's could be, blubbering out excuses in the face of David's rage. David forced calm, the calm he normally prided himself on, and nodded to the cook to release him. The cook hesitated briefly, but bowed to his employer's request.

"William Dobson, I no longer require your services. Leave my home posthaste."

He stalked from the kitchen without waiting for a response. He ignored Dobson's shouted curses, so incensed that he barely understood one word in seven. It mattered little. He'd already pushed the man from his thoughts.

His home was small, most of it dedicated to his school and his practice. He had rooms above for himself, his brother for whenever that man chose to visit, and a larger room with several cots for any students who decided to stay rather than travel home. The servants' rooms were in the attic and barely worth mentioning.

Though most of his patients were dead rather than alive, he still saw the occasional person who needed his help. It had been some time since he'd had to perform surgery like he'd done recently, and losing Olivia Miller had damaged his confidence more than he cared to admit. Saving Melly, however, had gone far in reinstating that confidence, that understanding of the human body and how it worked.

Having her sleeping in his room was something he didn't quite understand. Yes, she needed to heal. Yes, having her where he could monitor her progress was the intelligent decision. Yes, he could care for her better than her sisters. But none of that made logical sense...even if it all made perfectly logical sense.

He paused outside his bedchamber, hand raised to lift the latch. She'd been sleeping for the better part of an hour and it was unlikely she was awake now. Logically, he should turn and find his way to the students' chamber, allowing himself an hour or two of slumber before facing the day.

And he needed to inform Melly's sisters of her condition.

His hand dropped. They would still be awake, no doubt, awaiting her return, perhaps anxious beyond comforting at the moment. In fact—

The sudden pounding on the rear entrance was loud enough to wake the dead. Or the young woman recently rescued from that very state—or near enough that the distinction mattered little. David found himself bounding back down the way he came, determined to reach the door before the cook. There were only a few people who came to the rear door, none of them students.

As he passed his brother's chamber, that man emerged, sleep-befuddled and blinking owlishly. He'd managed to shrug into a silk dressing gown that would probably pay a goodly portion of his debt, though David doubted the blighter could be convinced to part with such a show of wealth and privilege. Just when would the nodcock accept that their father had not only died, but died with nothing to show for his constant speculation? The man had possessed no knack for gaming or trading, every investment he'd ever made coming to naught.

"What's to do?" James muttered, clearly having spent the better part of the night in the bottom of a bottle.

David ignored this. "Nothing of import, Brother. Return to your room and leave me in peace this day." Then he muttered a prayer to whatever gods might be listening. If only his brother would heed his request.

No such luck, damn James' scarlet enshrouded hide! He followed David below, heedless of his state of undress. David could have laid him low, but his exertions of the night, his assault on the porter, and the fact that he'd slept but hours in the last two days, left him feeling weary and drained of energy.

His morning visitors were already in the kitchen, having been invited in by the overly kind cook. David sent a weary scowl Henderson's way. His gaze fastened on five bedraggled misses, shivering in their rain-drenched cloaks and boots.

They looked much as they had the one time he'd met them all, when Miss Olivia Miller was laid to rest. He'd been given little opportunity then to really study the girls, and what Melly had told him about them before wasn't enough to determine which girl was which now.

"Miss Miller's sisters, I presume?" He expected no response and got none. Indeed, the one he assumed to be the oldest opened her mouth only to snap it shut again as her teeth chattered alarmingly.

David spun about, addressing Henderson. "Tea, man, quickly, and whatever food you can prepare to warm these young women. They are our guests."

Henderson nodded and David shepherded them to the long table near the fire. He settled them on the benches there, his mind trying to reconcile these quiet young misses as the ones who disinterred the dead for his school's use. They shed their cloaks, revealing dark gowns that would show little dirt, fingers uncovered and pale with chill. David couldn't determine their ages, though he knew them to be much younger than Melly.

Two identical faces, heavy and broad, young and lacking the beauty of the other girls, stared at him with twin bulldog expressions, lacking emotion. Another girl, older than the twins, pale and beautiful, bore a belligerent expression that David could only assume was directed specifically at him. Her dark-haired counterpart reserved judgment, it seemed, her features serene, her eyes watchful but calm. The youngest—or so she appeared—stared openly at him, a certain gleam in her eyes that David recognized. The youngest was a flirt.

Then her gaze slid behind him, widened just a touch, and slid back to him. He glanced over his shoulder, saw James, who seemed to have forgotten his state of undress, and returned his gaze to the girls at the table. He wasn't sure what to make of her reaction, and he had no time to fret over it.

"You are looking for your sister, Miss Melly Miller," he said, lowering himself into a chair near the door. Five heads nodded silently as each girl was handed a steaming cup of tea. "She is here," he assured them, feeling an inordinate amount of relief when he saw five pairs of shoulders ease with the news. "She was injured and is now resting comfortably."

The tension returned, as did the use of their tongues. Five voices filled the early morning silence, all saying much the same thing in different ways, every word but a few floating over David's head. He grasped one phrase that more than one of his guests uttered.

"You did this."

He resisted the urge to stand, defend himself. They had a right to expect the worst of him; he'd not hidden his feelings for their kind. His actions condemned him, and if he was completely honest with himself, he'd agree that it was his fault she now slept in his bed recovering from an attack that should have killed her, an attack that could have been avoided had he acknowledged that his feelings for her no longer resembled the contempt he'd first felt. He still refused to acknowledge anything more than curiosity and physical attraction.

Leaning back in his chair, he spread his hands. "I did not, though I did manage to stitch her up. Time will tell if she avoids infection." Their eyes widened with each word he spoke, mouths falling open in shock. "I do not know who attacked her, but she is not the first I've seen with such injuries and I suspect she will not be the last."

His explanation rendered them silent. He stood then, gesturing to the food the cook was then laying on the table before them. "Please refresh yourselves and after I will take you to your sister."

He exited the cozy room, grasping James' arm as he left, pulling that man along with him whether he wanted to go or not. He marched him to James' room, leaving him inside with the stern instructions to dress himself before venturing out again. "No, on second thought, dress yourself and remove your person to your own rooms, dear boy. I cannot tolerate your presence with this latest tragedy hanging over my head."

"I have no rooms," James admitted, not a shred of shame or embarrassment clouding his handsome features.

David had nothing more to say than "Indeed?" though in

his head he enjoyed the singular vision of throttling the life from James' unrepentant gaze. Truly, where had his utter calm and control gone these past weeks?

"Then by all means, make a home for yourself here. But I will put your lazy self to work, Brother, so do not think you will be able to continue to live the life of a baron's son any longer."

"But I am a baron's son," James protested, "as are you, so why should we not live as though we are? Do we not deserve to?"

David laughed, though mirth was not something he felt in that moment. It was amazement, plain and simple, at the entitled attitude he'd never before quite realized his brother enjoyed. "Deserve to? No, indeed. We are entitled to air, nothing more. Everything else, we earn. Father left us nothing, or near enough as to amount to nothing, and George washed his hands of us long ago. Thus the reason you come to me for money and not our saintly eldest brother. He would see you clapped up in debtor's prison before parting with a farthing."

With each word, James paled, as if finally realizing the situation he was in. When he opened his mouth, no doubt to protest, David held up one hand. "Enough. Dress yourself. I will return after seeing the Miller girls settled with their sister. Then I will inform you of your duties."

He left before James had a chance to form a sentence. He was through coddling his brother and regretted deeply that he'd ever done so.

As he walked away, his mind returned to Melly and her sisters and his less than gentlemanly treatment of them. It occurred to him that James wasn't the only one to have developed an attitude of entitlement.

Everything hurt. Her head pounded out a drumbeat she didn't recognize, mesmerizing in its monotony, while her ribs sent fire through her limbs. Blackness clouded her vision, but around the edges was dim light, something that confused her until she realized her eyes remained closed. She tried to open them, but the light along the edges brightened uncomfortably so she allowed them to close again.

A footstep reached her ears. Someone approached but at the moment, she couldn't remember where she was or who it could be. Her memories were cloudy, fear and panic overlapping calm and peace, acceptance that her end was nigh and the pain would dissipate ere long.

Warm hands touched her ribs, right where the fire began, hurtling a wave through her body that threatened to send her back into oblivion. Her muscles tensed against the onslaught of pain, eyes squeezing so tight that bursts of color appeared against the closed lids. Her lips parted and she would have screamed had she been able to manage anything more than the groan that emerged.

"Hush, love, you are safe now," a male voice whispered over her, calming her despite the pain. She could not ease her taut muscles, however.

The hands left her ribs, one smoothing over her brow, nonsensical whispers of comfort filling the silence. In moments, her tension eased even if the fire still burned her from head to toe.

Curious, she forced her eyes open. For several moments, she blinked against the light, which dimmed accordingly as her eyes became accustomed. She turned her head, just a bit, in order to find the voice that belonged to the hands that were once again probing at the fire in her ribs.

Doctor Melbourne?

She must have made some sort of noise. His hands stopped moving against her side and he rose to stand over her. "Miss Miller?"

She smiled, or at least she thought she did. She thought he might smile in return but his brow furrowed instead, as he laid a hand against her cheek. "No fever. That is good."

Then he did smile, a genuine smile of relief, one that reached his dark blue eyes and revealed a full set of teeth. Melly's breath caught as remembered wonder swept through her, masking the pain for the briefest moment. But the flame lit her ribs once more and the drum in her head resumed its incessant beat. Her smile became a grimace and another groan ripped from her throat as tears clouded her vision.

The soothing voice returned. "Be at ease, Melly," he told her, the sound of her name on his tongue oddly comforting to her ears. "Here." She found herself raised just a bit, a glass pressed to her lips. She drank the foul liquid it contained, trying not to choke. The doctor rubbed her back until the noxious liquid settled like a lump in her middle.

Melbourne returned to his seat, holding her hand in a firm but gentle clasp, his thumb moving over her skin in a soothing pattern. Gradually, Melly calmed again, blackness edging her vision as sleep battled for dominance. She blinked, hard, fighting the blackness, unwilling to allow her body to return to the oblivion she'd endured for—how many days?—unsure she'd return again, terrified if the blackness won, she'd be forever trapped in the nightmares that haunted her sleep.

A shiver snaked its way down her spine, her fingers convulsing in Melbourne's. Her eyelids drooped and she forced them wide once more, but something kept pulling them down, as if heavy weights had been placed on her eyelids. With one last, panic-stricken thought, the blackness won.

The next time Melly woke, the fire in her side was nothing more than a dull ache, easily ignored. The pounding in her head, however, was as strong as ever. She recalled some odd dreams, nightmarish creatures that stabbed her over and over, until her blood stained the cobbles. Did she scream once, terrified of the death these creatures brought? A soothing voice had calmed her in her nightmare state, sending her back into the blackest void where memory and dream ceased to exist.

Lifting her shaking hand to her side, she recalled something a bit less dreamlike, the memory of a man's laughter as she fell to the ground. That's when the fire started, in that moment, lighting up her side and catapulting her over the edge into an oblivion she was only now beginning to break free from.

How many days was it? She recalled the doctor, knowing she was under his care, the very same doctor who couldn't save Olivia. How much worse could it have been for Melly, had the man who hurt her been after something else, as in Olivia's case? Would she remember if her attacker had raped her?

She moved her legs, relieved they did as she wanted, but a bit disconcerted to realize she wore a man's lawn shirt—and nothing else—instead of something of her own. That unease lessened greatly, however, as she realized her legs moved quite comfortably with no soreness between them. But again, how many days had she been there, recovering from her attack? Surely long enough for such an injury to heal.

She set the worry aside for the nonce. There was nothing she could do now, and she couldn't know for sure until Melbourne returned.

David Melbourne set her mind to wondering other things, things she'd had occasion to forget with all that had befallen her and her sisters in the last fortnight. He didn't like them above half, yet he tried to help them. He worked to save Olivia and though he'd failed, Melly had a hard time blaming him. She blamed herself more. They could have left this life sooner, but she'd wanted a comfortable life, not just livable. She'd allowed her dreams to grow too big, allowed herself to think thoughts better left alone. What men would marry them, knowing what they were, how they'd earned their bread? It was far more shameful than selling themselves and most women never escaped that particular life. How naïve was she to think that they'd escape theirs?

Her deep sigh was cut short, the pain in her ribs reminding her to take shallow breaths. With an inward curse, she spread her fingers over the bandage, allowing the pain to ease back again, waiting until she knew she could manage it if she moved slowly and carefully. A little time. That was all she needed.

It wasn't her first serious injury, after all. Once, as a child, she'd made the mistake of trying to rescue a flea-bitten dog from a group of vicious boys. They'd left off beating the dog just long enough to teach her how wrong it was to meddle where one shouldn't, beating her until she thought she'd surely die, part of her wishing for just that. As she lay in the dirt, blood from a gash above her eye forming a small puddle beneath her head, she caught a movement from the corner of her eye. With one vicious movement, the largest boy slit the poor creature's throat. They walked away, laughing, less thought for the beaten girl than they'd spared for the dog.

Her mind refused to settle. She gazed around, taking in bright blue curtains the same color as the sky, blessed sunlight peeking around the edges to stream across the quilted counterpane. Melly marveled at the comfort of the bed beneath her, a feather ticking, no doubt, on top of the firmer horsehair mattress below. She'd only experienced such a thing once before. It was not a luxury she'd have thought the doctor would possess.

But James... Yes, James would own such a thing. He paid her £50 for a tumble, after all, so much more than a sane man would do. Clearly, he was well off. Her assumption that Melbourne was Quality seemed accurate.

She refused to think about James. He was nothing to her now, nothing but a mistake, a momentary lapse in judgment. If he was more gentlemanly than most, it only meant she'd been fortunate. She'd heard tales, seen firsthand, just how brutal "gentlemen" could be in their treatment of those they thought beneath them.

But what would Melbourne think if he knew? Did it

matter?

Disgusted with herself, Melly carefully pushed her body up onto one elbow to get a better view of her surroundings. Melbourne's own chamber, if she wasn't mistaken. She was certain the room wasn't considered large but the bedroom she shared with her sisters could easily fit twice in this chamber. Just how well off was he?

As if summoned, Melbourne entered. He strode purposefully to the bed, eyes huge at the sight of her propped up form.

"What the devil are you about?" he snapped. "You'll reopen your wound, do yourself further injury. Fool woman!"

"I'm weary of this bed," she complained, oddly comforted by his harsh concern. "I want to get up."

He braced a knee on the bed, putting his arms around her and easing her back. She watched his face, trying not to be affected by his physical nearness, though her heart kicked up a beat. He was strong, lean, his neat appearance attesting to his precise nature. His eyes met hers, anger, concern, fear, guilt, and an unexpected longing visible in them that made her breath catch. A vision of his lips touching hers sent heat racing into her cheeks and she finally looked away.

"You mustn't move," he muttered, as if he too labored under some strong emotion. Most likely the anger, she mused. "I didn't run myself ragged saving you just so you could kill yourself through your own fool actions."

A smile tugged Melly's lips. She couldn't help it. His concern did him credit, though his manner was far from comforting. Did he care for her, care if she lived or died? His attitude and actions seemed to indicate that he did, though she was unsure his contempt of her profession could be overcome.

"Raise your arm above your head," he ordered, his voice gentle despite the gruffness of the words. She did as he bid, curiously unabashed by her nearly naked state. He grunted his acceptance of her action, positioning the bedsheet so it would cover her while he drew the shirt up to expose her side to his intense gaze. His touch, though gentle, sent enough pain sweeping over her flesh that she tensed.

He paused, his eyes settling on hers. "I am sorry," he murmured, "if I hurt you."

Melly opened her mouth to assure him it was not his fault, but something in his gaze held her tongue. It wasn't just the physical pain she now experienced that prompted his apology. It was something more, something deeper.

"You no longer despise me," she accused, as astounded by the realization as he appeared to be. "You like me."

"Not through choice," he retorted, whipping his gaze back to the bandages as he carefully removed them. "You are...intriguing. Nothing more."

She laughed, the sound cut short on a hiss of what David could only surmise was a considerable amount of pain. Her arm came down around his neck, the tension in the limb pulling him close. It was only by great good fortune that he didn't land atop her, furthering her injury and placing them both in an embarrassing situation.

With one hand in the bedding by her wound and the other braced at her uninjured side, he managed to avoid just such a catastrophe. But his hands sank deep into the feather ticking, bringing them so close that his chest brushed hers. Fighting the urge to kiss her, calling himself several kinds of fool for even harboring such improper thoughts in their current situation, he struggled to right himself.

"As much as I enjoy being in your arms, my dear girl, you will need to release me," he informed her solemnly. He would have chuckled at his own lame jest if he hadn't been quite so aware of her as a woman and her precarious health.

Melly groaned, but a smile teased her lips at the same time. "Flatterer," she muttered, breath held against the pain.

David shifted his weight, allowing his right hand the freedom to grasp the fingers curling around his neck and unwind her arm. He eased her arm down, allowing her body to settle back. "Breathe, Miss Miller. Slowly, carefully, but breathe."

She nodded, then released the breath she was holding, the air hissing from between clenched teeth. Her body eased further into the bed. David held her hand, stroked her brow, and waited until she calmed. Then, as he had no choice, he revealed, "I must check your wound. I will be as gentle as I can."

She nodded and raised her arm once more. She didn't speak again and David could only surmise she needed all her concentration to avoid screaming or crying.

As he peeled back the linen covering her wound, he said, "You can cry," in as conversational a tone as he could manage. The idea of her crying ignited something in him that he might consider a protective instinct. He told himself it was only because she had no one to protect her and he was raised to believe women needed protection and it was a gentleman's duty to do so.

He firmly ignored the fact that his previous actions toward her put the lie to his theory.

"I have no need, sir," she whispered. "The pain is not so bad."

He didn't know how that could be but he said nothing, focusing all his attention on examining the slash that marred her nearly flawless skin. It looked much better, all signs of infection gone. As he prodded around the stitched up flesh, something snagged his attention from the corner of his eye.

A long scar, barely discernible, started below her ribs and disappeared beneath the fabric preserving her dignity. The scar was faded, something from long, long ago, but it hinted at a previous injury, one far more serious than the one he currently wrapped with clean linen. Curious but unwilling to quiz her about something that was none of his concern, he finished bandaging her wound, gently moved her arm back down to her side, and leaned away from the bed.

He reached for the laudanum he kept nearby. "You will need this for the pain," he explained, measuring out a small dose in a glass and adding water.

She shook her head. "No. No more. The nightmares are enough without that stuff to bind me to them."

"Nightmares?"

"He comes for me at night," she whispered, her voice so low David almost missed the words. "He taunts me, leaves me for you."

"Me?" His shock couldn't have been greater. "What have I to do with it?"

Her lips twitched, almost as if she held back a smile. But the pain in her eyes belied any humor she might have found in her situation. "He left me for you. *Another body for the doc.*"

His brows rose. Her words only served to verify his suspicion that the attack on her was directly related to her profession. But was it one of her own, or someone looking to avenge the theft of their loved one? He suspected the former.

There was little he could do at the moment and her nightmares were not the point. Her pain was. "Can you bear the pain enough to sleep? Sleep is most important now."

"I can. The pain is not so bad." She turned her head

away, toward the softly crackling fire that took the chill from the autumn air. "It was worse. Before."

"Before?"

Her head tipped back his way, wisps of sable hair sliding down her shoulder. "Have you never wondered at my odd views, sir? Why I feel less shame selling the dead than I do selling myself?"

That blunt statement of admission struck him in the chest, stealing the air from his lungs in a savage rush. He could not care what she did with her person, should not care. Yet he found himself caring deeply, anger and pity fighting for dominance in his mind. He shoved them both away, knowing he had the right to feel neither emotion. Melly was not his.

That thought caused more upset than he suspected. He must be sickening for something, a not unlikely occurrence given his recent habit of sleeping little in the hopes of seeing the saucy body-snatcher. What a fool he was!

"I will admit, I have wondered," he said now, mostly to fill the silence.

Her eyes closed, fingers tightening rhythmically in the blanket. She explained what happened to her as a child. "I'd have died, surely, had Pa not taken me straightaway to Doc Billings. He offered him as many bodies as Doc could ever want if he could only save me." She smiled sadly. "Doc saved me. Pa gave him two bodies in exchange and Doc said they were even." She paused, her dark brows drawing down in consternation. "I owe you some bodies, I think, for Olivia, and myself."

Eyes widening in horror, she choked out, "My sisters!"

"They are here and making themselves very useful. My home has never been better run, I assure you. Miss Sadie spends most of her time with cook, learning all she can, while Miss Ashlin has proven an apt assistant to me, in the running of the school. The twins care for the pony, my horse, and the cold shed where we store the cadavers. They seem quite content here."

Melly's pleased smile went far in lifting his own spirits. "And *Miss* Belinda?" Her teasing emphasis on 'Miss' would have amused him under different circumstances.

He scowled. "Miss Belinda is a trial. She insists on stepping out with a young man I cannot approve of."

Melly chuckled. "That is William and I agree, though telling her will do no good."

"I suspected as much."

Melly's eyes drifted shut. "They are safe here, then, safe from that life."

The amount of relief in her tone told him far more than he suspected she realized. But there was still something missing, a part of her explanation that she'd forgotten to include.

"You didn't say why you see no real shame in selling the dead."

"Didn't I?" Her voice was soft, like the tones of one

about to sleep. "Doc said the only reason he could save me was his use of the bodies Pa sold him. The dead saved me."

# Part 7:
# Death's Mercy

**M**elly struggled with the tapes on her sensible black gown. It was new, a gift from Doctor Melbourne. She'd never had the luxury of mourning, not an odd circumstance for someone in her position. The outward trappings of mourning were just that, an outward display. Why waste money on new clothes just to show others that you mourned the loss of a loved one?

But she could hardly refuse the gift when the doctor presented it to her, especially when he informed her that he'd made sure each of her sisters had a similar gown. They owed him much and if he wanted them to show the world that they mourned, so be it.

"Bloody 'ell," she muttered as her side took up a relentless throbbing. She paused, allowing her arms to drop to her sides, breathing through the pain. It would take many weeks, mayhap months to really get past the pain of healing.

She remembered just how long it took when she was a child, and being older now, much, much older, it would take longer, if she ever fully healed at all.

Sadie bustled in, her arms full of clean linens. "Melly! What are you doing up and about, you fool?" She tossed the linens on the bed and rushed to Melly's side.

Melly couldn't mask her relief. "Sadie! I need to get out. I'm headed to Bedlam if I don't leave this room!" She shifted so her sister could do up the tapes.

"You're not wearing your corset," Sadie observed, a smile twitching her full lips. "How positively scandalous."

"I nigh on fainted pulling my chemise over my bleedin' head," Melly pointed out with a scowl, angry at her sister for reminding her of her inability to even dress herself. "Corsets are the devil, so why should I start wearing one now?"

Sadie's answering laughter grated on Melly's nerves, but the other woman didn't insist on forcing her into the whalebone and cotton torture device, so Melly forgave her.

"Why are you up and about?" Sadie asked. "No one would be angry with you for staying abed a few more days, gain your strength."

Melly shoved her feet into her shoes, twinging at even the slight movement that required. "I am a useless, lazy creature and I refuse to be so anymore! I must earn my keep, just as the rest of you do."

It had been nearly a sennight since Melbourne declared her officially on the mend and informed her she would be able to leave the bed in only a few days. Her sisters felt some strange need to coddle her, keeping her to her bed until she'd finally had enough and attempted to rise of her own accord. She just couldn't bear it anymore.

Sadie said nothing more. She turned her attention to the bed Melly had just left, stripping it down and replacing the sheets with freshly laundered ones that smelled faintly of lavender. Where her sister came by lavender in the doctor's home was a mystery that Melly had little interest in solving.

As she stepped toward the door, Sadie asked, "Will you leave your hair like that? It's most becoming but scandalous."

"Stubble it, Sadie, do!" Melly snapped, her frayed temper getting the better of her. She'd already tried to at least tie the unruly locks into a tail, but the pain in her side was worse than when she'd pulled her chemise over her head. She was done with bowing to a bunch of rules she didn't even care for!

She left the room without another word to Sadie.

In the corridor she met Ashlin. The dark beauty seemed intent on her path, her features creased in thought as she wiped her bloody hands on an already stained cloth. Melly remembered Melbourne mentioning that Ashlin showed an affinity for his profession, even going so far as to assist him with his school. Melly wondered how the students felt about a woman having anything to do with their learning, learning right alongside them, in fact. Then she dismissed it. Ashlin's beauty allowed a great deal of leniency in many matters.

Melly paused, breathing harder than she liked, and waited for her sister to reach her. Ashlin glanced up, just as she would have trod upon her oldest sister.

"Melly!" Her gaze shot to the door beyond them, then back to Melly. "Whatever are you about?"

"I grow weary of my bed. I need to be busy."

"I do not believe David will allow such, Melly."

"David?" What possessed her sister to speak of the doctor in so informal a manner? And why did it cause a surge of pique in herself?

Melly wasn't sure, but she thought she saw a slight pink color Ashlin's pale cheeks. The light in the corridor was dim, however, and she couldn't be sure.

"Melbourne has no power over me"—she nearly choked on the words—"and I will not allow him to order me about."

"Then what do you hope to accomplish?" Ashlin inquired, calmly returning her attention to cleaning the remaining blood from her fingers with the damp cloth. "In what way will you be of use to the doctor's household if you do not take orders from the doctor?"

Melly said nothing. She'd allowed her own anger to talk her into a corner.

"Yes, Miss Miller," came a masculine voice from behind her, "I also wonder how you will accomplish such."

David stared at Melly, calmly awaiting her explanation, wondering at the fear that had coursed through him at the sight of her walking about as if she hadn't been stabbed not so long ago. She was a healthy woman, if not particularly young, so he'd suspected she'd heal rather quickly. But this —this stunning creature with the sable hair and flashing eyes who faced him with an indignant tilt of her head was not what he expected at all.

The silence lengthened as did the afternoon shadows.

The day had been mostly overcast, snow and wind adding a chill to the air that seeped into one's bones. Another reason he couldn't believe she'd left the warmth and comfort of her—his room.

His bed. Just the reminder that she'd spent so much time in his bed was enough to raise his temperature a goodly amount. His lust had been tempered by the thought of her injury, the fact that she was only there to heal from a stabbing most likely perpetrated by one of her own kind. Now, seeing her up, strong, healed enough to argue and fight, the lust surged back. He countered that with a healthy dose of anger and directed it at the cause. Her.

"Well? Have you nothing to say for yourself?"

"I have not."

Ashlin snorted a laugh and bobbed a curtsy in David's direction. "Sir, I shall withdraw and allow you to battle my sister alone." She left before either of them could stop her.

"Now that you've frightened my sister away," Melly snapped, directing her attention to David, "what have you to say for yourself?" Her lips twitched.

David laughed, truly amused. "Ashlin Miller fears nothing and well you know it." He smiled at her until the smile teasing her lips broke free, lighting her countenance. He held out his arm. "If it pleases you, will you join me in my office?"

Her dark brows rose. "For what purpose? Do you desire to ring a peal over my head for leaving the sickroom?"

"Indeed no," he affirmed, feeling a little foolish that he stood there with his arm out, waiting for her to take it, "there are things we must discuss. Nothing more."

Put like that, Melly saw little choice but to place her hand on his arm, just as a proper lady would do. Her fingers tingled at the contact. She ignored the sensation and allowed herself to lean on him just a bit as he led her down the stairs to his office below. She'd not realized just how tiring it would be to rise from her bed.

Melbourne settled her in a chair near the fire. He then bent to the task of stoking the fire, getting a good, warming blaze going before joining her. He lowered his tall form into the other chair, wincing a bit as he did so.

Melly frowned, savoring the blazing warmth as she leaned forward. "What ails you?"

"A silly tumble," he admitted after a moment of thought. "I stepped out to help the new porter retrieve another body from the storehouse and I slipped on the ice." He grimaced, his hand tightening on the chair arm. "Stupid, really."

Melly fought to keep the grin from her face. He seemed so embarrassed that she couldn't help but find it terribly amusing. It was clear he'd hurt nothing more than his pride, though he likely sported some colorful bruises as well.

"Yes, it's funny," he admitted, "but not to the point." She must not have hidden her smile as well as she thought. "I mentioned things we must discuss."

Melly nodded, truly unsure what he meant to discuss.

Her side still throbbed but it had settled to a dull ache. She leaned back, allowing the tension to leave her body in the hope that it would lessen the pain.

"Miss Miller—"

"Melly. I simply can't get used to anyone calling me Miss Miller," Melly inserted firmly, the dull ache in her side fading with each passing moment that she didn't move. Breathing carefully helped too, offering a little relief.

The corner of Melbourne's lips tipped up the slightest bit, as if he was amused more by her than what she said. "Melly, then." He settled back in his chair, his hands steepled together, brow furrowed in deep thought. "Melly, you have healed to the point that you no longer need my help. That said, you can return to body-snatching if that is what you desire. However—"

James Melbourne burst into the room, skidding to a stop when he saw them seated by the fire. "Oh! Bother. I didn't know the room was occupied." His gaze darted about, as if he suspected someone to be lurking just out of sight.

Apparently satisfied there was no threat, he grinned, the expression transforming his normally pleasing countenance into something quite unearthly, heavenly even. He sauntered forward, his eyes on Melly.

Melly stared back, unease crawling her spine at the mere sight of him. He had the appearance of any Society dandy with his bright waistcoat and form-fitting jacket. His doeskin breeches left little to the imagination and Melly, being Melly, couldn't help but remember what she was better off completely forgetting. But James Melbourne was a well-favored gentleman, the type of man that would cause many a woman moments of improper thought.

For Melly, guilt mingled with the heat, soon taking over. She recognized a predatory look in his eyes that wasn't there before she was injured. Before, she'd have doubted he even remembered her.

Stamping down the memories, the impropriety, Melly erected an emotional wall, determined neither man would divine her true thoughts.

"You are looking in fine fettle this morn," he directed at her, stopping beside her chair.

His eyes slid over her face. Melly didn't visibly react, though she felt the urge to slap him. She glanced at the doctor, who sat there silently watching his brother. David didn't seem to care that James was making a cake of himself with a body-snatcher, but in that, Melly was quite wrong.

David seethed. He'd become adept at hiding his emotions, however, except where Melly Miller was concerned, it seemed. But with James, he wouldn't reveal that the younger man's flirting was infuriating.

"Did you need something, James? We have things to discuss."

James glanced at his brother. "You will make Miss Miller an offer? Brother, I didn't think you had it in you."

James' grin irritated David. He had the brief thought that it was a shame he'd managed to pay off James' gambling debts. Should those debts still stand, some debt collector somewhere would be doing the dirty work for David. Mayhap rearranging his pretty face would teach James some humility.

David chanced a look at Melly. She showed no emotion, but there was something decidedly amused in her eyes as she met his wondering gaze. There was little he could do at the moment about her feelings, however.

He stood, facing his brother squarely. "James, please have the courtesy to leave us. What we have to discuss is no concern of yours."

James looked as though he'd object. But, with a final look at Melly, he bowed and departed, leaving them alone.

David resumed his seat, leaning forward, his elbows resting on his knees. He pondered how to word his request, how to make her agree to what he was about to propose. Seeing no other way, he simply blurted it out, like any gauche schoolboy.

"What I wish to discuss is your future. Here. With me."

# Part 8:
# Death comes Calling

There were few times in Melly's life that her frustration threatened to overcome good sense, but this was one of those moments.

The urge to stamp her foot, like some spoiled, rich little débutante, rose within her. David Melbourne stared down at her from his great height, his face lined with anger.

"You will do as I order you to do," Melbourne insisted, a muscle twitching in his cheek. "You work for me."

"I will not send her packing!" Melly insisted. "And you will leave her be."

"If you do not send her packing, I will," Melbourne snapped. "I cannot have a pregnant housemaid running about."

"You will not have a pregnant housemaid *running about*, yet you employ body-snatchers to manage your home?" Melly seethed. "There's a word for the likes of you."

"Hypocrite?" Melbourne's lips twitched.

Melly shook her head, then uttered a word she was quite sure the good doctor had never heard from a lady's mouth. His face colored up at her language, and a satisfied thrill shot through her. Instead of waiting for his response, she strode away, unable to recall the last time she was so angry.

No, she recalled another time quite well, long ago. Her father still lived and when he suggested she seek out an abortionist to rid her of the child she carried, rid her of Olivia, she'd exploded with rage. Terror might have taken up permanent residence in her brain at the thought of having a baby, young as she was, but the thought of seeking out a "cure" that left many a girl dying in horrible pain was even more frightening.

"The child is not to blame," she snarled to herself now, angry to have to relive the moments of her pregnancy. And all that only served to remind her of Olivia and how much she missed the bright, happy girl.

"Miss Miller!"

The doctor followed, his longer strides eating the short distance she'd managed to put between them. She quickened her pace, unwilling to endure another jaw-me-dead over the poor little housemaid she refused to let go.

It dawned on her that she'd have to lift her skirts and actually run down the corridor if she wished to evade him. Impossible! Even now, her side and chest began to throb, an uncomfortable reminder that less than one month ago she'd been stabbed. Making a last second decision, she darted into a room on her left, one of the few small, unused rooms in the house. She pushed the door shut behind her, but wasn't quick enough to turn the key in the lock.

"Melantha!"

Melly froze, too shocked to do anything but stare as the doctor entered the room. "What did you say?"

"Your name, fool woman. Do you often run away from a heated discussion?"

"Who told you my bloody name?"

"Does that matter?" When she said nothing, Melbourne threw his hands up. "One of your sisters mentioned it, can't recall which. Satisfied?"

"No," Melly snapped, fisting her hands at her waist. She stifled the desire to huff through the throbbing pain in her side. It radiated into her chest and neck. "I hate my name! My father was the last one to call me Melantha and that was when I told him of Olivia."

Melbourne had opened his mouth to speak, but at Melly's declaration, it snapped shut. Melly took advantage of his stupefaction to escape.

Melly's new cloak was much warmer than her old one, another gift from the good doctor. She seethed at all she owed the man. How was she to pay any of it back in any way other than flat on her back?

Though Melbourne had never renewed his proposal. For all she knew, his interest in her had waned.

She'd thought not a few weeks ago when they sat together and he asked her to stay. But he'd asked her to stay, not as his mistress, but as his housekeeper. She'd wanted to know what he needed two housekeepers for, as Sadie served that exact purpose. His shrug told her nothing other than he expected her to aid Sadie.

It was maddening, the situation she now found herself in. Being in debt to someone left a bad taste in her mouth. And she owed him on behalf of all her sisters.

A memory flashed through her mind. Miss Samantha, the young lady she and her sisters had rescued the year prior, had said something similar in regard to the debt she felt she owed them. Melly finally understood the miserable feeling of owing a debt.

Shaking the memory away, Melly strode through the streets she'd known since childhood. There were things she wanted from her house and the time away from Melbourne and his brother would provide a much-needed reprieve.

As she turned down the final street, mostly empty on this cold morning, she saw a strange, yet familiar figure. A nondescript man whose hat was pulled too low to make out his features, hurried away, giving no indication of having seen her. She didn't know him, but she'd seen him before, loitering near her home.

As she turned down the alley, a woman, hooded against the chill in the air, moved quickly toward her. It may have been nearly a year since seeing her, but Melly had no trouble identifying her.

"Miss Samantha!" Melly greeted with genuine delight. Odd to see the very person she'd just been pondering!

"Lady Gareth Bennett now," Samantha informed her with a happy smile.

"Made an honest woman of you, did he?" Melly teased, unable to help herself. "I am grateful you were able to distract him from having me taken up on charges."

"It was the least I could do after all you did for me."

Samantha smiled. "I have missed you, my dear."

She glanced around them, her smile fading as she reached for Melly's arm. "I am come to repay my debt," she almost whispered, leaning close. She tugged Melly away from the tiny domicile, her gaze darting about as if fearing discovery.

Melly could do nothing but scurry along with the fashionable matron, marveling at how well she looked. Her face glowed, strands of bright golden hair peeking out around the edges of her smart straw bonnet. There was an air of contentment about her, despite her odd urgency now. Marriage certainly agreed with her.

And if Melly's suspicions were correct, the slight heaviness in Samantha's cheeks indicated the impending arrival of a little one.

Melly grinned, pulling Samantha to a stop. "You're expecting a babe," she accused.

Samantha's face flamed. "Melly! Such a topic is most unseemly." When Melly said nothing, merely continued to stare expectantly at Samantha, that young lady threw her hands into the air. "Yes, yes, I am. Now, please come away with me so we may speak with you."

"We?"

Samantha's gaze darted about again. "Melly, please." She tugged Melly's arm, showing an unexpected strength.

Melly saw little choice. She nodded, pulling her cloak more securely around her. The cold was finally starting to penetrate, though she suspected Samantha's urgency was partly to blame for the shivers coursing her spine. She followed the young woman out into the main street, drawing to a halt at the sight of a waiting carriage.

"My lady, I—"

"Hush, Melly, and do not be so formal with me now. Come with me and Gareth will explain."

Stated like that, Melly saw little recourse but to oblige.

Melly's long walk home could have been avoided. Lady Gareth offered the use of her husband's carriage but Melly didn't want to explain to Melbourne how she came to be in a gentleman's conveyance. The man would probably assume she had a lover and ring a peal over her head the like of which she'd never before experienced.

Besides, she needed to think and what better time to think than on a long walk? She took roads she normally would not have, sticking with heavily populated thoroughfares, Sir Gareth Bennett's warning ringing in her ears.

"Someone was looking for you," he informed her with little greeting on his part. He'd never cared for her and still didn't, a reaction she could hardly hold against him, under the circumstances. He offered her no refreshment, saw her in a small room normally used to see traders, didn't invite her to sit and lowered himself into a chair just as soon as his wife sat. Bennett treated her as the lower being she was. She almost smiled at the apologetic look Samantha tossed her way.

"A man came here, somehow deducing that my wife knows you. He made some comments that frightened her, and she had me fetched."

His accusing glare cut Melly to the quick. "I would never endanger—!"

Bennett held up one hand. "Do not bother. Samantha felt the need to warn you, as the blighter did not bother to remain long enough for me to make his acquaintance." Bennett's glare settled on his wife. "She went to your residence today against my wishes."

Samantha glared right back. "You were too busy with your library to escort me. I took it upon myself to go and warn *my friend* of the danger she is in."

Bennett's lips thinned, but Melly saw the very real fear the man harbored. She couldn't fault the man for his protectiveness.

"I thank you for the information, but I fail to see the threat."

They turned as one to stare. It was Samantha, however, who responded.

"He asked for you by name. He told me you are a killer and the bodies you deliver are ones you killed yourself." Samantha paused, as if letting that bit of shocking information sink into Melly's head. "He said you'd come back and kill us."

Deeply shocked, Melly stepped forward, one hand outstretched in entreaty. "I would never—!"

"Of course you wouldn't," Bennett snapped. "Though you steal bodies, sickening as that is, you would not kill anyone just so you have a body to deliver."

"No, indeed," Melly mused, ignoring the contempt in Bennett's voice, "but I know of some who will."

And now Melly pondered that very thing as she traversed the busy streets making her way back home.

She stopped in the middle of the street, the shout of a coachman and shrieking horses not even registering in her stunned brain. She'd called Melbourne's residence *home*, just as if she belonged there.

It shouldn't come as such a surprise. Her sisters thrived in the home of David Melbourne, so much so, in fact, that one would never have thought they were once parasites living off the dead. Though money was far from plentiful in the doctor's household, he made sure each of the girls had three new gowns, two for everyday wear and one for finer things. Melly had yet to determine what occasion would warrant the need for such a garment.

Their day-to-day life certainly didn't require it. While she acted as housekeeper, her sisters retained the jobs they'd assumed while she healed. Full winter was upon them now, a bitter cold that filled her with thankfulness that they need not worry over accumulating bodies to support themselves. She remembered many a winter that they returned with fingers nigh frozen and legs so cold they could no longer feel them. Melly couldn't begin to express her gratitude to Doc Melbourne for his kindness.

Well, there was one way she could, but he no longer seemed interested in a tumble. Besides, a niggling feeling —one might call it an instinct—told her that if she gave in to the good doctor nothing would be the same. It would change her. She'd grown too close, too fast. There was no logical reason for her feelings, yet there they were.

Now she brought a danger she couldn't control, and it would land right on the doctor's doorstep if she didn't soon take action to stop it.

With a shiver that had little to do with the cold, she finally moved from the street.

Two hours later, David paced before his table, completely ignoring the beauty who worked on the body that lay there. Ashlin hummed as she worked, some little tune he didn't recognize. It was an oddity that he'd already become used to, a beauty with bloody hands, elbow-deep in the latest body to grace his anatomy table, a jaunty tune on her lips that clashed with the seriousness of the situation.

She showed no embarrassment and never had. But he

suspected each of these young women held a certain prosaic view of life, one many in his circle would consider quite scandalous. He paused in his path from the door, his eyes on her as she worked.

His mind, however, was focused entirely on her absent sister. Melly railed at him with no fear of reprisal. She was an oddity in her own right.

Many housekeepers wouldn't hesitate to send a pregnant housemaid packing. He should have assumed Melly would object, considering her past.

When he'd asked her to stay on as a servant, it wasn't the question he'd really wanted to ask. No, his mind wouldn't focus on anything but keeping her at his side, where he could watch her and know she was safe. He wanted her much closer than that, but she'd made it painfully clear that any interest in that was solely on his side. Thing was, he wasn't sure that was all he wanted from her anymore.

He opened his mouth, wanting to determine what Ashlin knew of her sister's prolonged absence, when the very woman he fretted over strode determinedly into the room. Trailing along behind her was Sadie, Belinda, Emerald, and Ruby. Ashlin glanced up from the body, giving her sisters a warm smile that faded as she took in the serious expressions that faced her.

"What's to do?" she asked, straightening. She took up a cloth and began wiping the blood from her fingers, the movements automatic, unhurried, methodical.

Melly's gaze went from Ashlin to Melbourne, sadness filling her eyes as she looked at him. David couldn't begin to imagine what she searched for in his expression but he took a step forward, concern and a certain feeling of dread coming over him.

Melly shook her head, taking a single step back. Her words were for her sister, but her gaze never left David's.

"We must leave, Ashlin. Immediately."

"No."

# Part 9:
# Flirting with Death

The single word shattered the silence caused by Melly's announcement. She'd expected a bit of resistance from her sisters but it wasn't one of their voices that broke the silence.

All eyes turned to Melbourne, mouths snapping shut. He stood there, arms crossed over his chest, his gaze steady on Melly's face and no one else's. Light streamed through the window, but Melly couldn't read the emotion blazing in his eyes. Anger, surely, was part of it, and perhaps a bit of betrayal at what he might view as abandonment. Guilt surged up in her. Her gaze dropped for just a moment as she attempted to gather her resolve.

Drawing in a deep breath, she met his gaze again. "We must. Crouch will not stop and he will not stop at me. He will kill us all."

At the word kill, Melbourne stepped forward, the movement casting his face into shadow. His hands fisted at this sides, his entire body tense. "Crouch? Who is Crouch?"

"Another body-snatcher," Ashlin supplied helpfully from her place at Melbourne's side. Her hands were still at the moment, no longer wiping away the evidence of her activities in the lifeless body open on the table behind her, though traces of blood lingered here and there on her pale skin.

She hadn't moved to join her sisters and if Melly read her stance properly, she wouldn't. She'd made her choice and her new love of physicking, of learning the mysteries of the human form and learning how to help her fellow man, would take first place to her family now. Melly's heart sank at this evidence of familial disloyalty, though she couldn't help but feel a certain measure of pride in her sister's choice.

Melbourne frowned heavily, his partially shadowed features adding a certain malevolent quality to the expression. His body eased just a bit, as if Ashlin's prosaic tone assured him the threat was not as great as Melly implied. "As I suspected, all this melodrama is due to one of your own."

Melly bristled under the accusation, but told herself he couldn't possibly know the kind of man Crouch was. If he did, he would never say such a thing to her, or to any of her sisters.

Sadie saved her from a response, the younger woman stepping around her to challenge Melbourne. "We are nothing like that bloody bounder!" she snapped. "He would slit his own mother's throat and sell her to one of *your* kind. *We do not kill.*"

A tense silence ensued, in which the sisters waited for either Sadie or Melbourne to back down. Melly hoped Melbourne would realize just how harsh his assessment was. And she fought the sinking feeling in her middle, the despair that he would believe such a thing, let alone voice it.

"Very well," the doctor allowed, the faintest tightening around his mouth indicating he felt at least a touch of embarrassment over his undeserved judgment, "he is not the same. But what does he stand to gain by murdering the lot of you?"

Melly didn't respond right away. She studied Melbourne's face, hardly able to believe he was so naïve as to not realize Crouch's ultimate goal. As the silence lengthened, she leaned forward. "You."

Melbourne wasn't sure Melly could have said anything that could have stunned him more. "Me? How am I a factor in any of this?"

"If we are gone, that leaves the way open for Crouch to deliver to you," Ashlin provided, her gaze steady on the last bits of blood she cleaned from her fingertips. "It has long been known that though small, your school needs far more bodies than most." She glanced up for the briefest moment, as if to assure herself that he was indeed listening. "After experiencing how you teach, it is no wonder." Her attention returned once again to the task of making sure every trace of blood was removed from her hands. "Crouch would benefit greatly from gaining your business."

David's gaze flicked from Ashlin to Melly and then over each of the girls' faces. He saw fear and worry, a little despair, and a frightening amount of deadly intent in the eyes of the twins. He nearly shuddered, though he knew it wasn't directed at him. He had to stop these young women from leaving if for no other reason than to prevent the twins from taking matters into their own capable hands.

"And what do you propose to do?" he asked Melly, shaking off the disturbing sensation that allowing them to leave would be the worst thing for everyone. "And will leaving fix your problems? If you go back to your life amongst the dead, he will only try again to...*kill*...you."

He stumbled over the word, resisting the suffocating fear that rose up in him at the memory of her bleeding form on his table. Hardening his resolve, he pointed at Melly, then each of her sisters. "He will remove you all, if you are correct in your estimation of his character." He stalked forward, standing toe to toe with the eldest Miller sister. "You would take your sisters back to that, living in the night, stealing the dead, always looking over your shoulder, afraid of what might lurk just around the next corner?"

Melly's lips thinned. "I would never willingly endanger them," she snapped. She muttered some choice invectives calling his parentage into question, but David wisely refrained from commenting or even revealing that he knew exactly what she so vulgarly suggested. Part of him wanted to chuckle at the sight of a beauty like Melly Miller even knowing such words. She was intriguing, a contradiction of everything he'd ever learned about women.

Instead, he focused on the real issue at hand. "Yet that's exactly what will happen if you leave here now."

Another tense silence ensued. The primary combatants stared each other down while the bystanders gazed on in amusement. Ashlin shot a knowing look at Sadie who smirked in return. Neither said a word, and both realized there was more to the situation than even their eldest sister realized.

Melly considered Melbourne's claim. What he said might be true. Her sisters were in danger no matter where they were, but the danger would certainly increase if they returned to body-snatching. If they returned, Crouch would still view them as what they undoubtedly were: the one thing that stood between him and a considerable sum of money.

Even realizing the truth of Melbourne's statement, she couldn't help feeling the need to flee. "What do you propose we do?" she challenged.

David straightened, her choice of words sending a shaft of realization through his muscle-tightened form. "Do not leave. Stay here with me."

Her breath caught. It was almost a repeat of an earlier conversation, one in which Melly found herself agreeing to toil alongside her sisters as another of the doctor's servants. Honest work, to be sure, certainly lacking the stigma of a resurrectionist, but unsatisfying to a woman who viewed her employer in a most improper light.

She stilled the quickened hammering of her heart, straightening her spine just a touch to give herself some much needed confidence. "Continue on as your servants?"

"No," David stated, his gaze never wavering. He reached for her hand, disentangling it from the front of her cloak. One strong tug pulled her from the relative safety of her sisters, nearly tumbling her straight into his arms. "You stay here, as my wife, and Crouch can go hang for all I care."

In the brief, stunned silence that followed, Melly searched David's features, a sudden rush of feeling threatening to send her into a proper swoon. His eyes held an intensity that surprised her. Though he'd certainly displayed an inordinate amount of emotion since they'd fallen into his life, she'd never beheld quite as much emotion as she did in that moment.

Her fingers tightened in his. Was it possible? Did she truly hear him speak the very words she privately longed to hear? Could it be true? Elation rose within her, joy and wonder at the thought of all her dreams coming true and with a man she admired.

And just as quickly as the elation had risen, it fizzled. She couldn't see a way around her past, couldn't see accepting the offer of a gentleman who didn't know everything about her. It shouldn't matter, and she never considered that it would, but now, in the moment of her triumph, she realized just how ridiculous that was.

But as she opened her mouth to respond, the silence shattered.

"Bloody hell!"

Melly and her sisters remained in Melbourne's exam room, Ashlin shrugging her shoulders and returning to the body upon the table, while David roughly ushered James from the room.

It was a miracle the younger man kept his mouth shut until David had him out of earshot of the women. He didn't care what his brother thought of his decision, but he wanted to spare Melly the humiliation of James' inevitable repudiation.

David may not have thought through his impulsive decision to ask for Melly's hand, but the more he thought about it, the more he liked the idea. She needed him and, oddly, he needed her. He needed to protect her, and even if that meant taking care of her sisters as well, he was more than willing. Hell, if she asked him to give up his school and spirit her off to some remote cottage in the country, he was willing.

He almost stumbled as he moved to sit behind his desk. It was a strange realization to have about a person, especially when contemplating giving up the one thing that made him feel whole, the one thing that made him feel as if he was more than just another son of a lord, born into wealth and entitlement. His work made him feel as if he could give something back to the world, helping future generations of surgeons understand the human body to a greater extent.

Could he really walk away from all of it for a woman many of his peers would call no better than she should be?

He could. But he didn't think it was something she'd ever ask of him.

And there was nothing his brother could say that would change the way he felt about her.

"You cannot marry her, David! Think of the scandal," James stated, caring little that anyone within a half mile could hear him. "She's a body-snatcher." When his brother just sat there, nothing in his bearing indicating the disgust he must surely feel at the reminder, James grew desperate. "She's a whore!" There had to be something he could say, some way to get through to David, make him see how insane he was to consider the body-snatcher as a bride.

David still failed to react, though he leaned back and crossed his arms over his chest, his jaw tightening imperceptibly. Had James been anybody else, he'd have missed the slight change in his brother's bearing. So he knew he was on the right course. Melly's past selling herself made a much greater impact on David's calm than the reminder of her cadaver theft. So it followed that...

When he hit on the one thing that would make his brother listen, James almost winced at the vulgarity of it. Yet, he had to try. He had to make David see just how foolish it was to wed Melly Miller.

Inwardly cringing, James sat, the large mahogany desk the only thing separating them. He drew in a breath, knowing his next words might get him killed.

"I've had her myself."

# Part 10: Return of the Dead

The short, derisive laugh James heard behind him had him spinning toward the girl who uttered such an indelicate sound. It seemed David had failed to properly latch the door when he'd shoved James into the small office. Sadie Miller stood there, one hand on her generous hip, all her sisters arranged behind her.

Melly's face glowed stark white in the pale light streaming in through the window. He turned his head from the hurt in Melly's eyes, only to encounter Sadie's. He closed his eyes, unable to face the accusation he saw there.

He'd just told his brother that Melly Miller was completely unsuitable to join their family, going so far as to admit that he'd paid for her favors himself. And apparently, he'd admitted that in front of the Miller sisters, the beautiful Sadie amongst them. His heart sank further, as if that was possible.

He turned back to David, sure he'd be facing the pointy end of a dueling sword. But David hadn't moved. He still sat behind his desk. His eyes were glued to Melly's face and James couldn't read his expression, couldn't tell if he believed him or if he'd choose to follow the inappropriate urgings of his heart.

Sadie gestured to James dismissively. "What does that matter, Mr. James Melbourne? You've had half the lightskirts in London. The other half avoid you for fear of the pox."

James' face flared red, a muttered invective his only response. Sadie laughed, a certain bitterness in the sound that her listeners had never heard before. James knew the source of her upset and couldn't help the unfamiliar feeling that assailed him. It was an emotion he'd never felt before this day. Shame.

An uncomfortable silence fell. James fought the urge to fidget. He prayed, for the first time he could remember, for a miracle to intervene, save him from the hell he'd created for himself and everyone around him.

His salvation came from an unlikely source. "May I have a moment with Miss Miller?" David asked, his voice low and even. His fingers clenched around the quill on his desk.

James sidled out the door, hoping he'd done enough damage to make David think about his decision to marry Melly. He avoided Sadie's eyes as he left, firmly suppressing the rush of emotion he had every time he looked at her.

As he moved past Melly, James chanced to glance her way. The look on her face as her gaze went from David to him, the way the late morning light hit her dark eyes, struck a memory buried deep inside. There was something, some inkling that he knew her, and not just the memory of her caresses the prior year. No, this was something older, something so shocking he stumbled over his own feet, nearly ending on the floor. He grabbed for something, anything to keep him upright, his fingers closing around the arm of the nearest girl.

That girl happened to be Melly.

Her eyes landed on him and she stared. He knew then that she'd always known exactly who he was, as soon as he'd again entered her life. She knew.

"Release me," she whispered.

James nodded, too shocked to do anything else. He stumbled away to find a bottle of something to erase the memories again.

Melly's attention turned to her sisters. "Go. I will be well. Doctor Melbourne would never hurt me."

"Do you believe that?" Sadie asked Melly, though her eyes remained steadily on James as he stumbled away.

Melly glanced over her shoulder at the younger of the Melbourne brothers. Her eyes followed his progress for a brief moment before returning her gaze to Sadie. "Go to him, Sadie. Forgive James and me, and go to him. I fear for his sanity now." She'd never seen James act in such a way, positively drowning in shame. A man as self-absorbed as James having his wrongs paraded before him without mercy might not react as well as someone more grounded.

Sadie hesitated. "I care not what becomes of James Melbourne."

Melly laughed softly. "Love, I see the way you watch him when you think no one is looking. I do not believe he will make a good husband, but I also do not think he should be alone with his demons. Keep him from harming himself. He will listen to you."

Sadie left without another word. Ashlin frowned at Melly. "You utter such brave words, Melly. Our lives resemble nothing of what they used to be, yet you move with the changes even while you attempt to subvert the inevitable. David will not marry a woman who lay with his brother, especially when he learns the daughter you buried was really his niece."

With that truth lingering in the air between them, Melly's sisters strode away. She fought the urge to follow them, reluctant to face the truth of her sins.

How could Ashlin have discovered that truth? How had James, for that matter? Melly'd seen the realization in his face, knew he finally remembered her. At long last.

He remembered her as the whore he'd made use of the previous year, and now, Melly knew, he remembered her as the little whore he'd used thirteen years prior to that.

She'd fought the urge to cast up her accounts more than once since she'd come to live in Melbourne's residence, terrified James would realize their past was more than a single tumble a year ago. The fact that James spent little actual time in the house helped ease her fear a bit, but the few times they came in contact with each other kept her nerves on edge. It had taken her some time to accept that he didn't remember their sexual encounters.

It sickened her now, to think on it, to realize just how low she'd sunk. Indeed, why did she not just admit to one and all that she was exactly what she never wanted to be? A whore.

Her mind flew back, all those years to the moment she'd first seen James: golden curls, sky-blue eyes, the chiseled features of a god, and enough charm to thaw the Thames on the coldest winter days. Melly saw him as the physical manifestation of everything her young heart had dreamed. He was the man she'd marry, the man who would take her from the dark life she lived.

Hope was a dangerous thing for one such as her, and that day it was Melly's undoing. She didn't know what he was doing so far from the upper echelons she assumed he hailed from, but when he saw her, his smile blossomed, calling forth an answering smile in her. He offered her money, and Melly, stupidly awed by the golden beauty before her, accepted, barely understanding what it was she accepted.

He was only a few years older than her, barely a boy himself at the time. It was her bad luck that a child resulted from that encounter, and it was her stupidity, her naïve longing for love that placed her in his arms again thirteen years later. What a foolish, foolish woman she was!

Though James had been the ideal her heart desired, at least what she'd always dreamed of in her girlish fantasies, he was nothing compared to David. Her heart stuttered at the mere thought of David, at the thought of a life with him, children with him. Where James had been a moment of excitement, a moment of passion—quickly over and deeply regretted, David was stability, protection, trust, and—dare she think it?—love.

But it couldn't possibly be, not after the things James revealed to him and certainly not after she told David of Olivia's true parentage.

Straightening her spine, she turned and prepared for battle. If David had heard Ashlin's perspicacious utterance, he gave no indication. Melly selfishly hoped the subject of Olivia's father would not come up, but her hopes were moot. She needed him to know, and she needed him to reject her. Instinct told her she lacked the strength to reject him.

She finally entered the room, forcing one foot in front of the other.

"Close the door," David instructed, still seated behind his desk.

Melly did as bid, daring a quick glance at her employer. He slowly rose to his feet, an odd gesture of respect given the circumstances. Her heart betrayed her at the action, a simmering hope growing in her breast that despite all her sins, he might still accept her, still want her as his wife.

"You heard what James said," David began. Melly saw his hand clench, then ease as if forced. "Is there truth in his claim?"

She nodded, unable to find her voice. He sighed, shoving his hand through his dark hair. "I do not know what to say, Melly."

She nodded again, feeling a bit as though her head

would nod itself right off her shoulders. She forced her lips to part, dredging up enough voice to answer the accusation...and add to it.

"There is more." Her voice was a mere breath of sound, barely audible to her own ears. She cleared her throat and tried again. "There is more."

His eyes narrowed, a frown pulling down the corners of his lips. Memories flashed in her mind. She remembered the excitement of James' touch, the naïve belief that maybe he'd love her now, now that they were both grown. Shame crawled up to settle in her chest.

Then she remembered David's kiss, feeling as though she'd come home. Her place was with him, of that she had no doubt. But she wasn't sure his place was with her.

Shoving past the feelings, the memories, and the shame, she told him the whole truth. "You know Olivia is—*was* my daughter." Pain lurched her heart, tears gathering in her eyes. She held them back. "Olivia was my daughter and your brother..." She paused, unable to speak around the lump in her throat.

David took the need from her. "James was her sire." No question lingered on the words. His gaze bore into hers, as if trying to divine the truth of her claim. "Are you sure?"

Melly's hands tightened on her cloak. Sardonic laughter rose within her, threatening to break forth in a bout of hysteria the likes of which the good doctor had surely never seen. If a woman lays down with one man, as a matter of course she'd certainly lay down with too many to count! As unfair as it was, she understood his assumption, but she couldn't stop the hurt his question caused.

And she saw no reason to defend herself. If believing her to be a lightskirt would give him some peace in his decision to turn his back on her, so be it.

"I cannot be sure," she lied, raising her chin and forcing sincerity into her words. "You know how whores are. We can't remember one john from t'other."

Sadness mingled with a flash of anger in Melbourne's eyes just before he glanced away. He may have guessed she lied, but he said nothing of it. "I know I asked for your hand, Miss Miller, but under the circumstances..." He paused, his eyes searching hers as if for some denial from her, some explanation he could accept. With none forthcoming, he sighed. "I think it best that we part ways."

Melly's heart sank, lungs deflating. She forced back a wave of desolation, forced back the moisture that wanted so desperately to fall from her eyes. "Of course, sir." She nodded for emphasis, more for herself than for him. "I will leave posthaste."

She bobbed a respectful curtsy, but didn't immediately depart his presence. Steeling herself, she inquired, "Might I beg a favor of you, sir?" He nodded, reclaiming his seat behind his desk. "My sisters...Ashlin in particular."

He nodded again, saying, "Your sisters are welcome to stay on here, should they wish it." He studied her face a moment, then added, "I do not believe they will wish to stay, however."

It was enough. "I want them to have the choice. All they ever wanted was to be able to choose their own paths. Thank you for that."

She left him then, before she could give in to the pleading in her mind, the tiny voice beseeching her to beg his forgiveness, to give her the opportunity to prove to him that her past was her past. She wanted... she *needed* him to understand that things were not simple, especially for someone like her.

The quill in David's hand snapped. Decades of upbringing wouldn't allow him to marry a woman who'd sold herself, no matter the reason for such an action. Decades of pride wouldn't allow him to marry a woman his brother had intimately known, a woman who bore his brother's child.

Not even if that woman haunted his dreams, caused a willingness to abandon everything he loved, and made him want to murder his own sibling.

He wanted to follow her out. He needed to do something for her, not having forgotten the threat that still lingered over her and her sisters. If he no longer desired to take care of her and they decided to follow their sister out, the very least he could do was provide them with enough money to get them out of the body-snatching life.

That thought spurred him from behind his desk. "Miss Miller! A moment!"

She paused, turning slowly to face him. David resolutely ignored the hope that sprang into her tear-filled eyes. "Sir?"

"I would like you to take this." He reached for a set of small silver candlesticks on a table near the door. He should have sold them himself long ago, but he'd just never gotten around to doing so. "Take these. They should fetch a fair price and make it possible for you and your sisters to leave the graveyards in your past."

Her tears disappeared as she looked from the candlesticks to his face. "You hope to salve your conscience? Why?" Nothing in her tone suggested she condemned him for the possibility, just a curious observation.

"I hope to keep you safe. Even if—" He broke off, unable to finish the thought. His traitorous heart urged him to throw caution to the winds.

He shoved the offering into her hands and stepped forward, almost against his will. His hand touched her face, curving around her cheek for one last caress. Silky tendrils of midnight hair swept over his hand. Her eyes slid shut, one shuddering breath leaving her lungs. "I wish things were different, Melly," he whispered. "I wish I was different."

Her eyes opened. "I understand," she said. Then she reached for him, heedless of the candlesticks in her hands, sliding her arms around him to pulled him close. She kissed him, her lips barely touching his, the softest caress before she released him forever.

Hands dropping to her sides, fingers white around the candlesticks, her sad smile touched him in a way nothing else had. "I apologize. I just wanted...something to remember."

David couldn't leave it at something so simple, not after all they'd been through. As she turned, he grasped her arm, pulling her fully into his arms. Too many emotions surged through him as he leaned in, plundering her lips until they were both breathless and shaking with a need they could barely contain. The candlesticks fell, ignored as they struck the floor. Melly's fingers dug into his jacket, heat seeming to burn into his back from a touch that couldn't possibly cause such a sensation through his many layers of clothing. But he felt that touch, drawing her as close as he could, molding her form to his and marveling at how perfectly she fit him.

Feeling his control slipping, David released her. The look in her eyes told him she felt the same, desire beckoning them to take that step, the one that would see them both assuaging the raging need they felt for each other. He stepped away before he did the unthinkable.

Melly touched her lips as David stooped to retrieve the

forgotten candlesticks. "Take care," he told her, finding little else he could say.

She simply nodded and took the offering. He watched her walk away, fighting the ache in his chest. He wanted nothing more than to go after her, tell her he loved her.

He wanted to tell her none of it mattered.

But he would be lying.

# Part II:
# Escaping the Dead

The Miller sisters silently packed their things to leave. They chose to go with Melly, even Ashlin who stood to gain so much more by staying. The doctor insisted they take all the clothes and things he'd provided for them, having no use for them himself. Melly was grateful, as it was one less thing to worry about when they were trying to make new lives for themselves, but the weight she carried deep inside would not be lessened with distance.

As they set off, Melly did not want to return to their tiny, dilapidated hovel near the graveyard, though there were things they needed to gather there before they could move from the city forever. The girls trundled along behind her, thick shoes on their feet and heavy, warm cloaks keeping the biting winter chill from their bodies.

"Melly," she heard Ashlin whisper at her side, "I'm sorry David turned us out."

Melly heard tears trembling on the words and she felt her chest constrict. "You could have stayed, love," she murmured, careful to keep her voice low. "Doctor Melbourne would continue your education. You could be a doctor yourself someday." They both knew how unlikely that was, but at David's side, Ashlin would at least be allowed to practice the art she loved so well.

"I could not let you leave alone," Ashlin retorted.

Melly laughed, a hint of actual mirth in the sound. "Hardly alone, love. Do you think the others would have stayed as well?"

Ashlin nodded. "I do. Had I chosen to stay, the twins would have as well, finding much satisfaction in the lives they have made for themselves with Melbourne." Her gaze lingered on the stout girls, Melly's eyes following. Ashlin then glanced at Belinda. "David managed to talk some sense into Belinda's head and she gave her footman his marching orders. Her new beau is far more pleasing." Her gaze slid to Sadie. "I need not tell you that Sadie's heart remained back there, though she'd deny that if you asked."

Melly's heart sank with every word her sister uttered. She'd destroyed her sisters' chances at happiness, true happiness. Desperate, grasping for anything to heal a portion of her guilt and anguish, she asked, "But you would like to marry, would you not, Ashlin? We would all like to marry. One day." Though she doubted she'd find a man who would overlook her past, considering a man she loved, who loved her, couldn't overlook it.

Ashlin frowned. "I've thought for many years that marriage would be pleasant, Melly. A home of my own, children. But now..." Her sigh came from deep within. "Now, I've found something far more valuable to me."

Melly stopped and her sisters stopped with her. "Why did you not stay with Melbourne? None of us would have condemned you for it, and if our sisters chose to stay, more happiness to you all."

"Melly," Belinda spoke up, "we are family. You have done so much for us. We would like to help you."

The twins nodded but said nothing.

Melly's shock ran deep, mingling with a sense of outrage. "Why do you say these things now?" she demanded. Her bag slipped from her fingers, settling at her feet with a dull thud. "Months ago you desired to make your own choices. Yet now you follow me, intent on doing as I tell you.'"

"Things change, Melly," Ashlin soothed. "We made choices, we made mistakes, and we lost Olivia." She paused, taking a deep, steadying breath before she continued. "We know that you've always cared for us. And now we wish to make that clear to you."

Sadie nudged Melly's shoulder. "If you say we go, we go. If you say we must return, we must."

"I can't go back," Melly whispered. "He doesn't want me."

The girls surrounding her burst into laughter, startling Melly. "What ever has come over you?"

"Doesn't want you?" Sadie grinned. "Love, that man can't think when you walk into a room. He wants you and none other."

Melly stared at each of her sisters in turn. They spoke the truth, she knew, but they didn't seem to understand the full extent of her sins. Passion, desire, lust, or whatever one chose to call the physical pull David experienced when near her was quite simply not enough to overcome all that had come before.

"Sisters, I know you mean well, but there are things you do not—"

"That Olivia was our niece, not our sister?" Belinda asked calmly.

Melly's shocked gaze swung to her youngest sister. "How did you—?"

"We are not flats, Melly," Emerald and Ruby said in unison.

Ruby went silent as Emerald added, "We've known for nigh on six years."

"Admittedly," Sadie continued, bitterness coating her words, "we did not know James sired Olivia."

"We are well aware that the man who chose to take us in was not sire to all of us, either," Ashlin stated matter-of-factly. "Once we realized that, it wasn't difficult to determine Olivia wasn't his child, though it was longer before we realized she was yours. What you thought you were protecting us from is still a mystery, I admit."

Melly's mouth opened and closed. Black lined her vision, air refusing to replenish her deprived lungs. An ache in her side developed, reminding her she'd suffered a life threatening injury not too long ago. Memories surfaced, ones of her father taking in yet another child the mother claimed was his even though that was impossible at the time. She had tried to protect the girls from the truth but now, in light of everything that happened, she saw just how pointless her actions were. Newer memories replaced the ones of her father, memories of James and what he'd once meant to her, the dream of him that shattered with the birth of her child. More memories rose to overshadow those, however, ones of David, his smile, his touch, the way he sought her out, even the way he vexed her. Those remembered emotions played through her mind as if to taunt her with just what she'd squandered. She grasped her nearest sister.

Sadie stepped forward, slapping Melly soundly on the back. "Breathe, you twit," she scolded, a certain fondness to the command belying the harshness of the words themselves.

Presently, Melly's lungs began working again, allowing air in and out as was proper. She steadied, allowing her sisters to pull her into a darkened alley where they could not be viewed by prying eyes.

"You must...go back," she told them between gulps of air. "You must...leave me...and return."

Five voices rejected her plea. She held up one hand, the other pushing into her side to alleviate some of the pain. "A moment." The words were barely more than a breath of sound, but her sisters heeded her wish, each falling silent as they waited for her to speak.

After a few moments, she straightened. Drawing in one deep breath, she proceeded to order her sisters about, just as she always had.

"You will return to Melbourne. You will tell him that I

let you go, that you are there to take up the lives you made for yourselves there, the lives you deserve." She swallowed the tears, swallowed the fear and the loneliness that already tried to choke her. Steeling her resolve, she looked each girl in the eye. "You deserve the lives you made there. Go back. Take up where you left off. Allow your past to fall away. The twins will continue their work, Belinda will marry her new beau, Ashlin will learn her new trade, and Sadie—"

"Sadie will what, Melly?" Sadie demanded, hands on her hips and scowl on her face. "Sadie will return to James Melbourne and forgive him for his wrongs? Sadie will tell him his deplorable behavior is in the past?" Her voice raised in pitch until she nearly screamed her frustration. "And then what, Melly? Sadie will become his kept woman?"

"At the very least," Melly muttered, "Sadie can tell him she carries his child."

"How—!?"

"Oh, come now, Sadie!" Melly snapped, angry and frustrated. "I've seen the way you watch him and the way he watches you. No one here was fooled by the way you avoided each other. I'm sure even Belinda noticed, despite her distraction with her own beau."

Belinda nodded helpfully, a teasing grin stretching her lips as she gazed upon her older sister.

The urge to scream rising within her, Melly changed the subject with a lifted hand. "You will return, all of you."

She braced herself. They would plead, beg her to rescind her command. But she also knew they would do it.

They surprised her. This time, they made no objection. They simply took up their bags and turned back the way they'd come. Melly watched them until they disappeared around a corner. Then, turning her back, she walked away, heart heavy, and tears streaking her cheeks.

David spent hours dissecting a body while two of his students looked on and answered questions as he asked them. He used the opportunity to think, not about the open man on the table—what thought was required when the man was clearly old and lacked a mystery to go with his death?—but about the girl who'd fled his life to return to God only knew what.

He'd determined he was a fool mere moments after she departed. How could he let the woman he loved walk out without so much as even trying to make a life together?

There was little he could do about it now. She was gone and he knew his chances of finding her were limited. She now possessed the financial means to leave her old life behind, to disappear into the vast city.

Sighing, David dismissed the students. They bowed respectfully and departed, allowing him the peace and silence he craved in that moment. He set about cleaning up the cadaver, his movements methodical, requiring little to no thought.

A commotion at the back of the house had David cleaning his hands and moving to the door before he even realized the sounds he heard. Joyful cries of welcome from the cook could only mean one thing. The Miller sisters were back.

He stifled the joy that rose within him. Melly. He missed her smile, her outspoken nature, her efficiency. He missed the way he'd catch her watching him, the way he'd watch her when she wasn't aware. He missed her family, the light and laughter they brought to his staid domicile.

And it had only been hours since they left.

Things were just not simple anymore, not since Melly entered his life. He found someone in her who didn't look down on him for the choices he'd made, though he'd certainly looked down on her for hers.

Shame filled him. What a lowly, despicable creature he was! He condemned her for a past that wasn't entirely her fault. He condemned her for her upbringing, refusing to acknowledge that in her circles she and all her sisters were pure as the driven snow.

What a fool he was! He glanced around the room, seeing the same things he saw every day. The exam table, occupied by the dissected cadaver, surgical instruments in varying states of cleanliness, and towels both clean and soiled, candles on every available surface, late afternoon light streaming in through the window. Things that usually filled him with satisfaction, a sense of purpose, left him cold, alone. He was alone with the dead.

Shaking off his morose thoughts, he made a sudden decision, one he was determined to never regret. To hell with his family. To hell with James and that man's inability to control his baser urges. And to hell with David's own pride.

He marched from the room, intent on telling Melly immediately.

The kitchen rebounded with laughter, feminine and masculine. David entered, fully expecting the silence he received. But he didn't expect the absence of the eldest Miller sister.

"Where is Melly?" He could read nothing in their expressions. "She did not return with you." It wasn't a question, rather an obvious fact that he couldn't help giving voice to.

Rage surged through him. He wasn't sure who he was angrier at, Melly for her cowardice or himself for his stubborn pride. Perhaps it was his own cowardice.

"Where is she?"

Sadie stepped forward. "She didn't say where she'd go. But I suspect she returned home."

"Home? With Crouch seeking her blood?"

The girls could do nothing but nod. Ashlin remained impassive in that odd, quiet way she had. Her eyes darted over him, pausing ever so briefly on his hand that still held the bloody towel. With a slight curtsy, she left them, no doubt to return to the very room he'd just left. The girl's love of his life was confusing, even to him.

"Is she mad?" he demanded, his anger all for Melly now.

Sadie laughed. "Oh, yes, sir, that she is. And you are the one to blame."

"Placing blame will not save her neck," David inserted with a sharp glance at Sadie. "I will retrieve her."

The girls fell silent as death. Only the soft murmur of whatever cook had bubbling on the stove relieved the silence.

He could make no sense of their silence and so left them to it. He shrugged into his greatcoat, slapping his worn beaver onto his head, and exited by way of the kitchen door, ignoring the sudden chatter that erupted after his departure.

His feet led him only a few steps before he realized one very important fact: he had not the least clue where Melly's home was.

Inhaling as though all of life frustrated him—as indeed it did—David turned about, fully intending to return and humble himself before the Miller sisters enough to glean the information he needed to retrieve their sister.

As it turned out, he needn't have bothered. James rushed out, Sadie on his heels.

"Doctor Melbourne!" Sadie shouted. "James knows the

way. He shall show you."

David had no desire to be in James' company for the length of time it would take to find Melly. And he certainly didn't think Melly would appreciate his presence.

Before he could protest, James spoke up. "Do not try to dissuade me, brother. I am to come along and keep you alive." His glance shot back to the young beauty on the doorstep behind them. "Or my life shall be forfeit should I return without you."

David suppressed the smile that threatened to tip his lips. Sadie would lead his brother a merry dance and David couldn't help but feel the fool deserved every bit of torture she chose to inflict.

Saying nothing, David continued on his way, headed in the direction he'd seen Melly go many a time. James caught him up, blessedly silent, merely pointing when a change in direction was required.

It wasn't far and both gentlemen stopped short several feet from the little hovel.

"What the devil happened?" James asked.

David shook his head. "Perhaps nothing," he offered, having no real idea just how the Miller sisters lived. He made his way to the tiny domicile, noting the missing door and the broken glass in the one tiny window. His gaze shot up and down the street, taking in the decided lack of windows in most of the hovels. "I suspect Crouch wanted to make sure Melly and her sisters couldn't return."

"Crouch?"

David chose not to enlighten his brother on the hatred the other resurrectionist bore the Miller sisters. Indeed, once David located Melly and convinced her marrying him was the only logical choice, none of them would have to fret over Crouch's jealousy ever again.

James' eyes left the domicile long enough to catch a movement in the shadows. Darting after the fleeing shadow, he disappeared into the alley beyond.

David started after him, fearing God only knew what, certain his brother would never emerge and wondering just what propelled him to chase after some vagrant. Rounding the corner, he came to a stop, mouth dropping.

"Melly!"

Melly didn't return home right away. She knew the danger and was unwilling to risk it even for the few little keepsakes she'd managed to save over the years. No, she went to the one place she knew she'd find shelter, even if the master of the house was not best pleased with her.

Her knock was answered promptly, as was proper in a well-run household. The butler looked her up and down, sniffed with much disdain, but stepped aside to let her by. He may not have approved of her, but his mistress did, and that secured Melly's admittance.

She kept her eyes lowered, finding it went much further with lofty servants if she maintained a certain measure of subservience. "Is her ladyship at home?"

"I shall check," was the automatic reply.

He left her in the foyer, her gaze still locked on the toes of her unfashionably sensible footwear. She didn't raise her head until a pair of far more fashionable slippers came into view.

"Melly!"

Her gaze locked with Samantha's. Tears bubbled in her eyes, spilling over to stain her cheeks.

"Oh, Melly!" Samantha crushed her in her embrace, trying her best to soothe her overwrought friend. Melly released all the misery she'd kept tightly inside, feeling an odd sense of relief to be there, with her one and only friend.

It was several minutes later that the women were ensconced in a small withdrawing room, one that appeared less for show and more for comfort. Melly breathed in her surroundings, feeling a certain amount of relief, though something still held her in its grip. A pervading sense of loss consumed her.

"Tell me all, m'dear," Samantha soothed, her tone washing over Melly. "You are heartbroken, that I can tell."

Melly's smile was tinged with bitterness. "Does it show so well?"

"Only to one who has known such misery. My Gareth wasn't always the charming, forgiving man he is today."

Melly snorted before she could stop herself. "Forgive me, my lady," she blurted, "that was most disrespectful!"

Samantha only laughed. "You forget to whom you speak. I am well aware my husband's forgiveness does not extend to you as yet. Give him time, Melly, and he will. I promise."

Melly's heart sank. Of course residing with Samantha was out of the question. Sir Gareth would never allow it. Especially while his wife was breeding.

Pushing to her feet, she said, "I am sorry to have bothered you. I will take my leave."

"Nonsense!" Samantha rose right along with her. "I will not hear of it. You are here for a reason and that reason involves a certain doctor with whom you've been living. Tell me it's not true."

"It is true."

"Then explain why you are here and not with him."

The command was soft but firm, and Melly found herself spilling out the whole sordid tale. When she revealed Olivia's true parentage, Samantha gasped in quite the best melodramatic fashion. Melly fought the urge to roll her eyes at her friend's display.

"You can see it is all for naught. He cannot forgive what I've done and I've no right to ask that of him."

Samantha said nothing, merely studying Melly's face for a long while. Apparently deciding it was useless to argue, she asked, "What shall you do now?"

"I do not know. That is the dilemma I now face. I have money but no way to set up my own household. Would Sir Gareth possibly help me?"

"He might. He may bear no love for you, but he does appreciate the help you've been to me." Samantha shrugged, a resigned smile settling on her lips. "We can but ask."

Sir Gareth's help was shortly after obtained, and he left immediately to speak with his man of affairs. He promised she'd have a residence by the end of the day. Melly couldn't help but smile at his clear desire to avoid her presence, and ensure her swift removal from his home.

It was while she stood alone in the withdrawing room—Samantha having excused herself to tend to some domestic matter—that she realized she'd forgotten something very important. She had money, but the majority of it was still in an ugly pot, hidden under a loose floorboard in the bedchamber.

"Bother," she muttered to the empty room. She'd have to venture home after all, hoping Crouch wouldn't be watching. If he caught her alone again, she'd end up on Melbourne's table for certain.

Firmly ignoring the pain clenching her middle, Melly strode from the house and out into the street. Avoiding all major thoroughfares, she made her way home, good fortune smiling upon her until she emerged from the street and saw two men lingering near her house.

"David?" The name tumbled from her lips before she could stop it. Panic swept her spine as she turned about and ran. Every fiber of her being urged her to escape before he saw her.

Strong fingers wrapped around her arm. Her heart jumped into her throat and then plummeted. Unable to break free, Melly capitulated. "Will you never be gone from my life, James Melbourne?" she sighed.

Her words brought her captor to a halt. She couldn't read his expression, but the shame of earlier was nowhere in sight.

"If David has his way, no, Miss Miller, you will not." His gaze swept her features. "Much as it would please us both to go our separate ways."

Melly had no opportunity to respond. James took her arm and continued, bringing them face-to-face with David Melbourne.

Many thoughts went through David's head. Oddly, it was the way the late afternoon sun lit blue streaks in the tendrils of midnight hair escaping her hooded cloak that spoke to him, igniting a desire that he'd not expected in the heat of his anger. He snatched at the fading anger, gathering it close in his mind, reminding himself of the danger she was in and her complete lack of willingness to fight for that which she desired. The anger flared, saving him from making a cake of himself right there in the street.

He took a step closer, hands clenched at his sides. James released her arm. David assumed she'd attempt to run but she stood her ground, her features set in stone, eyes respectfully lowered. David took that as a good sign. Perhaps she was willing to listen to reason.

But reason wasn't what his love-addled brain chose to shove past his lips.

"Do you love me?"

Her stony expression cracked. "I do, of course I do."

His fingers dug into her arms, pulling her body closer to his. "Then tell me why, Melly, tell me why you didn't fight. Tell me why you cowered in shame and slunk away like a beaten cur."

Melly's ire rose, her face lifting from his waistcoat buttons to focus on his eyes, so close to hers. "Fight? For what, pray tell? What would you have me do, Doctor Melbourne? Would you have me beg your forgiveness for things that happened long before I met you, long before I loved you? Do you think I should marry a man who will always look at me with contempt, resenting a past I cannot change? Do I deserve that? Do you?"

"And if I assure you your past is not you, and something I will willingly forgive?"

Annoyance flickered to life, but Melly snuffed it. "And can you forgive that I wouldn't change my past even if I could?"

His startled expression told her far more than he intended, she was sure. She struggled to pull away but his grip tightened. She winced, and he immediately eased his grip, though he still didn't release her.

"No, Melly, I understand. I have no right to forgive something that had naught to do with me. Your past is yours and what you did brought you Olivia, a darling girl from all I've known and heard of her." He gave her a little shake as she attempted one more time to free herself. "I understand."

His words sent a wave of peace over her, but guilt snuffed it out. "I should have told you about your brother," she whispered, firmly ignoring the fact that the very man she spoke of lingered barely beyond hearing distance. "I should have told you of the mistakes I made, that I'd...*sold*"—she nearly choked on the word—"myself. I foolishly hoped you'd need never know."

David was silent for a long moment, his thoughts somewhere Melly couldn't begin to fathom. Finally, with a glance over his shoulder at James, he asked her, "I wonder, Melly, if you truly sold yourself."

Melly's brows drew down, confusion taking over. "What can you mean? I accepted the money James gave me. What is that if not selling myself?"

"I know my brother and I've come to know you. I cannot envision you doing so, though I am well aware that many women who would never do so are yet driven to it. My brother, as a youth, was not a discerning young man."

Her confusion cleared. "That is true. My head was turned by his charm when I was a girl. The payment then was a shame I dared not share with my father until I discovered I was carrying James' child."

"And last year, when you saw him again?"

She sighed. "My dreams of escaping this life, of having a proper family...I grew reckless. Though I never lay with any other man, I stupidly thought..." She broke off, shaking her head sadly at the mess of her life. "I thought marriage was still possible. When I happened upon James one day, I remembered him. I thought mayhap he'd remember me and take me from all this. I thought—"

David shook his head, cutting off the words she didn't want to say, the words he clearly didn't want to hear. "It matters not." He pulled her fully into his arms, hugging her as if he could prove his words by simple force of will. "Can we not simply leave the past in the past?"

She pulled away, trying to think and unable to when he held her so close. He wouldn't allow her to fully retreat, his fingers again gripping her arms as she stepped out of his embrace. "You will come to resent me."

"Who are you to predict the future?"

Melly sighed in defeat. "Not a prediction, David." His given name slipped from her lips without conscious thought, and though she knew how unwise it was to address him with such informality, she couldn't regret it. "Logic. Tell me it is not possible. Tell me and I will believe you."

His hands gentled on her arms, resolve flickering in his eyes. "I cannot tell you that. I am no more a soothsayer than are you. But I do love you and find myself miserable without you. Mere hours without your presence and I cannot think. What I feel for you is not sane, it is not logical, it is not predictable, but it is without end. And I pray you feel even a small measure for me of what I feel for you."

"Feelings change, David." The words escaped before she could stop them. "And people are unforgiving. I am known to some of your associates. The scandal would never die."

"Then we shall make a life for ourselves elsewhere."

His words were quiet, firm, utterly devoid of hesitation. Melly's lungs stopped as she searched his face, knowing he couldn't possibly mean what he was suggesting. She must be mistaken! He loved his work, he loved teaching others the things he'd learned. How could he consider leaving it all behind? For her?

Melly's heart melted. "You cannot mean that?" she whispered, taking a single step closer. "Your work is everything to you. How could you live without it?"

His fingers eased, leaving her arm to brush a stray curl that refused to stay in the knot she'd forced her mane into earlier in the day. Heat tingled through her.

"For you, Melly, there is nothing I wouldn't do."

Melly cocked her head to one side, deeply moved but curious at his declaration. "Would you disown your family?"

As soon as she spoke, she knew the answer. He would. He would give James his marching orders, or disappear without a single word to his own brother. He would denounce everything he knew, all for her.

He opened his mouth to respond, but Melly pressed her fingers to his lips. "No, I would never truly ask such a thing of you. It was unkind of me to suggest it."

"And yet, I find I would do that, for you." His words tickled her fingertips. She dropped her hand. "But in doing so, you would lose Sadie. Her heart will not be turned from James, more fool her, and well you know it."

She knew that. Sadie was a stubborn creature, the worst of all the Miller sisters. And Melly could well understand her fascination with James.

"Melly, allow me to protect you. Allow me to love you. Give this scandalous affection we bear for each other the chance it deserves."

What could she really know of the future? How much greater was the regret of never knowing, never allowing their love the chance to overcome the obstacles life had put before them?

Finding no words to match his, she did the next best thing. She shook herself free of his hold and grasped his coat in both hands. Pulling him close, she pressed her lips to his, pouring every ounce of love into her embrace. May her father forgive her, but Melly was done. The darkness was finally at bay and the dead could no longer hold her.

# The End

*Death Becomes Her continues...*

# the Devil she Knows

a tale of loss
...and love

Jaimey Grant

# Chapter One

*London 1812*

Sadie Miller did not take life for granted. As the daughter of a resurrectionist, and having herself been a thief of the dead, she knew just how fleeting life was, and knew without doubt that any given moment could be her last.

Thus it was with prayers trembling on her lips that she screwed up her courage, her strength, and her will, centering all of it to her lower extremities, pushing forth the life she'd carried inside her for the past seven months. Exhausted, she fell back on the bed, panting, chest heaving with the force of her exertions. The room lingered in silence for several moments, then the midwife's concerned grunt burst through Sadie's consciousness.

She forced her tired body up onto her elbows, trying to see around her own legs to the women who'd helped her labor. "What? My baby?"

Her eldest sister, Melly, frowned over at her. Leaving the midwife to her task, she approached Sadie's side. "The child is so small and he does not breathe. He may yet, but —"

Sadie nearly came off the bed in her desperation to reach her child. "No! He will live! Let him live!"

Melly held her back, expending little effort in doing so as Sadie's strength was spent. "Love, there's nothing you can do. Lie back, be at ease. Mrs. Blume will do all she can."

Sadie fell back, desolate but determined to remain hopeful. Silence reigned, intermittently disturbed by a sound from the midwife. "What of David? Can he save him?"

Melly's gaze flashed to the closed door. "I will see. Perhaps he can." She turned to leave, but at the last second returned to the bedside. "Do not try to rise. You have lost much blood and there's nothing you can do for your son."

Sadie remained stubbornly silent. Melly shook her arm. "Promise me, Sadie. Promise you'll stay put."

Sadie nodded, knowing Melly's stubbornness rivaled her own. She wouldn't go for her husband until Sadie promised.

Melly disappeared a moment later. Sadie laid there, listening to the midwife laboring over the lifeless babe. Sadie willed back the tears, willed back her despair until it was known for a certainty that the babe would not live. Someone would have to tell James and she wasn't even sure where he was.

David burst into the chamber, Ashlin hard on his heels. "Stand aside!"

The midwife jumped, doing as ordered. She returned to Sadie, taking care of her while the doctor took care of the infant.

Sadie closed her eyes, wishing she could close her ears

as well. She did the next best thing. As a child, she'd sung songs in her mind, managing to lose herself in the tune in her head, blissfully unaware of the turmoil around her. It was a miracle she'd not died due to inattention at some point in her life, but God, or whoever dealt the cards, wouldn't allow it.

A gurgling cry shattered the unnatural quiet. Sadie came out of her trance, almost coming off the bed as well. The midwife scolded her in a halfhearted manner, her own relief at the sound seemingly as great as Sadie's.

"David? He lives?"

No more sound came. Melly turned away from her husband and sister, returning to Sadie's side. "I'm sorry, love. He was just too small."

"No." There was no sound to the word, just a helpless moving of lips. Sadie felt a piece of her heart die. She tried to retreat into her head but the music had left her.

"Sadie, this is not the end. You can overcome this."

Melly's words barely registered, but Sadie dredged up enough strength to respond. "Women lose babies every day in our world. Remember Letty Wilkes? She birthed dead babes one after the other until the final one took her too."

Her bitter words made her sister flinch. Melly's hand went protectively to her rapidly expanding middle and Sadie felt a moment of remorse for inflicting unintentional pain on her beloved sister. But she couldn't care at the moment. Her womb was empty, her heart was cracked, and she had no one to hold her and tell her all would be well. She had no husband, no lover, no one.

Her eyes slid shut. She heard movement as everyone left her to her rest. Sadie succumbed to her exhaustion, sleep taking her beyond the heartache.

# Chapter Two

James Melbourne led a charmed life. Through misstep after misstep he'd emerged on top, unharmed. With a bit of charm and his handsome face he could talk his way out of any situation. Nothing stood in the way of what he wanted.

But war was not something one could charm. James had suffered right along with the ugliest, most crass creature, an injury to his leg and the resultant fever ending his bout of good fortune. Though, in all honesty, having escaped death was probably as lucky as one could get.

As he lay senseless, the fever taking over his body again, he longed for home, longed to see the family he'd left behind. He'd never been a sentimental type, but fighting for one's life had a way of turning one into a simpering milksop.

And, simpering milksop that he was, he missed home. He missed England's dreary rain and London's suffocating fog. He missed his overbearing, sanctimonious brother David, and David's equally judgmental wife.

Then there was Sadie. Beautiful Sadie, low-class and foul-mouthed, damning him one moment and pleasuring him like a courtesan the next, the woman he loved and couldn't have.

He'd had to leave England, but there were some who didn't see it that way. Sadie Miller probably despised him and he could hardly blame her. But marriage was out of the question. James would make a terrible husband and Sadie should have a husband worthy of her loyalty.

And David deserved happiness, something he would never have if his wife constantly fretted over being in the vicinity of a man she'd once had carnal knowledge of.

He groaned. What a fool he was! He should have stayed, fought for Sadie the way David had fought for Melly.

A small hand patted his shoulder. He wanted to reach out, offer comfort to his comforter, but he couldn't acknowledge the action. His groan drew the attention of a nurse, who rushed to his side. Her ministrations were less gentle than they could have been but James simply ignored her. His fever wouldn't allow him to focus and he gave up, letting sleep claim him once again, memories of Sadie the only image he could conjure.

A month later James finally returned to England.

He stood on deck of a small vessel, hand firmly wrapped around the head of a cane. He'd limp forever now, the surgeons in battle lacking the skill his brother could boast. He'd already come to terms with that, though, finding far more to fret over with a recurring fever that could take his life whenever it willed.

His fever left him in peace for a time, at least. He was

warned of the likelihood of its return, but he cared not. England's shores beckoned.

A small hand slid into his. He glanced down at his companion, offering an encouraging smile. The girl smiled back, but her eyes soon returned to the shore that had yet to show. Her peaceful expression, her calm acceptance of her new lot in life, went far in settling his own anxiety. Indeed, without little Isabel, James wasn't sure he would have survived.

Isabel squeezed his fingers, as if she knew his thoughts, as if she could sense his unease.

Just before he'd been laid low with shrapnel in his leg, he'd found Isabel. The child wandered onto the battlefield, collecting the few wildflowers that had yet to be trampled underfoot, seemingly unaware of the horror going on around her. James blinked, unable to believe his own eyes. A beautiful little thing with olive skin and dark hair, she'd skipped about in her stained yellow dress, a bright, unsullied spot amongst the blood and carnage.

Thundering hooves brought James out of his stupor and he'd glanced beyond her. An English soldier bore down on her, as far as James knew completely unaware of her presence. He'd reacted then without thought, throwing himself on the nearest horse and riding to her rescue. As he swept her up into his arms he realized it wasn't just flowers she collected. The little pockets of her smock were filled with bits and bobs she'd looted from the dead.

He glanced around, seeing no one else. Most looters waited until the aftermath to sift through the dead in an effort to secure valuable bits to sell, not wanting to risk their necks. The more gruesome of the creatures went after teeth, knowing they would fetch a pretty price with the toothdrawers, some even helping the injured on their path to their maker in order to secure them.

This little girl seemed to be alone, no parents off looting while she learned to do the same. It explained why Isabel was in the midst of a battle, alone and oblivious to the danger.

Pity welled up. He'd taken her with him that day, putting her in the care of one of the camp followers until he could send her to England, to Melly and David. Through his rudimentary Spanish and her broken English, he'd managed to learn she was an orphan, her parents killed in one of the many skirmishes that plagued her country. She would be five in little more than a sennight. James smiled at her pride in that, his memories of his younger years reminding him that he'd once been as innocent, maybe more so.

His own injury happened before he could send her off, so she stayed with him, cared for by the women who made themselves available to the soldiers. He'd battled his fever and when he woke, it was Isabel who stared down at him, a sweet smile creasing her cheeks.

Thus he found himself homeward bound with a child at his side, a child he'd grown to love as his own. It was an odd turn for a man like him.

Though Isabel had managed to distract him from his sorry existence, he still thought of Sadie Miller. Her fair features plagued him worse than any fever. Memories of her, the fall of golden hair down her silken back, her laughing eyes, and pouting lips, caused him many a sleepless night. And remembering just how generous a creature she was did nothing more than remind him that he was a selfish child, always on the lookout for his own gratification and no one else's.

Isabel squeezed his fingers again, smiling up at him before darting across the deck in the direction of their cabin. Shaking away the useless recriminations, he followed, further cementing his determination to change his wastrel ways, better his life.

And then he would convince Sadie Miller she should marry him.

# Chapter Three

There was nothing for it. Sadie needed to decide what she'd do, but there was a problem. She didn't know.

She couldn't continue to stay on with David and Melly. They would never ask her to leave, but the house was crowded and would only become more so as children began to arrive. Sadie wasn't sure she could be there for the children, the pain of losing her own little one a constant ache in her chest.

She could go to her youngest sister Belinda and her husband, but they had a much smaller home. It would not be long before they began having children, taking what little space they had left.

The twins still resided with Melly and David, and Ashlin had no plans to ever leave her life as David's apprentice in his school of anatomy. Sadie truly had nowhere to go and her traitorous heart was glad of it. She wanted to be right there, in David's home, when his brother returned from the war, a hero, the kind of man David wanted him to be.

The problem was Sadie loved James even when he was a selfish, unapologetic reprobate. His charming, charismatic personality drew her like a moth to a flame, tempting her to lose herself in his laughing blue eyes. She'd done just that, and now mourned the child they'd created together, the child he still knew nothing about.

Ashlin entered the room, her face blank, eyes unfocused as she was lost deep in thought. Sadie stared at her, experiencing a rare surge of jealousy.

Ashlin Miller had one goal in life: become a doctor like her brother-by-marriage. It would never happen but it didn't stop Ashlin from pursuing that dream with everything she had in her. She didn't allow anything or anyone to sway her from her goal. Sadie envied her that ambition, envied the desire she had for something other than a man and children.

"Do you need something from me?"

Ashlin glanced up, clearly startled. "I did not realize you were here," she murmured.

Sadie wasn't surprised. She stood at the window in David's tiny office. Bookshelves lined the walls, filled with tome after tome of medical mumblings. Sadie had no interest in anything on the shelves and only preferred this room for the view afforded through the window.

She could watch the busy street below. Like a love-starved war widow, desperately awaiting the return of her husband, Sadie gazed through the rain-streaked pane. But there was no husband for her. Indeed, James was the last man any woman should marry!

Ashlin cursed softly, drawing Sadie's eye. Her sister swiftly exited the chamber, a large tome clutched in her hands. If she didn't pay attention she would run into—

"Oomph!"

Sadie couldn't prevent the smile that tipped her lips. Ashlin's lack of attention must have sent her straight into a wall.

Still smiling, Sadie returned her attention to the window. Her thoughts turned inward, fully occupied with memories better left forgotten. Finding more pain than peace in such musings, she sought to find the music that always saved her. Alas, it seemed to have left her completely, ever since the night her child died.

So the memories dominated, causing the constant ache in her chest to grow, choking off her air. Her fingers grasped the window sill before her. She wanted the music back, and fought to regain it. Why did it leave her now, just when she needed it the most?

So caught up was she in her internal struggle she failed to hear the entrance of another. In fact, it wasn't until the newcomer placed a hand on her arm that Sadie realized she was not alone.

She spun, ready to inflict an injury on her assailant that he'd not soon forget. But he forestalled that plan with a swiftness she'd not expected. Something clattered to the floor as his other hand shot out, dragging her forward to slam into his chest. She glanced up into her captor's face and all the breath left her lungs.

"Jamie!"

His lips crushed hers, evoking all those old emotions, transporting her back to the last night she'd spent in his arms. Raw desire pulsed to uncontrollable life, sending her wits spiraling into oblivion. She returned his embrace with wholehearted abandon, sliding her hands into his rain-dampened curls, reveling in the heat his touch ignited in her flesh.

So caught up in the wonder of being in his arms again, she barely noticed when he backed her across the room. Her legs came up against David's desk, the sensation jarring her wits back for a brief moment.

It was a moment she desperately needed. James' hands had managed to loosen her hair, undo the buttons on her gown, and drag her skirt up her leg almost to her thigh. A moment longer and she'd have let him have his way with her. Again.

The man certainly knew his way around a woman's garments! Sudden disgust for herself lending her the strength she needed, she shoved at him.

He stumbled back, falling to his knee with a hiss of pain.

Sadie dared not approach him, not with her heart hammering in her chest and her limbs shaky as a jelly. She braced herself against the desk behind her, struggling to calm her erratic breathing, watching James Melbourne as he shoved himself up, leaning heavily upon a nearby chair. It was then she saw the cane on the floor.

Her gaze shot back to his face. There were lines there that hadn't existed before. He carried a certain weight on his shoulders now, something that he'd never had to endure. He'd changed in the months he'd been gone.

As her breathing steadied, he regained his feet. And then

he smiled, that all-encompassing, knee-weakening grin for which he was well known.

Sadie steeled herself against the coming onslaught of charm. "James Melbourne, what the devil do you do here?"

"I am come home from the war, injured and in need of succor."

"Find it elsewhere."

He took one halting step forward. Sadie wanted to ask what befell him in Spain, but he spoke before she could form the words.

"Oh, come now, love," he crooned. "Did you not miss me?"

"Like the pox!"

The infuriating makebait's smile widened. He clearly disbelieved her claim. And how could she convince him otherwise when she could tell her appearance put the lie to her words? Her cheeks felt hot, her chest heaved, and her heart beat a rapid tattoo against her ribs. The bounder still affected her as no other, making her wish things were different, that they could somehow be together. But that could never be, not while he remained the world's worst example of manhood.

Beyond that, however, was the inescapable truth of their difference in station. He was the younger brother of a baron and she was the bastard daughter of a resurrectionist. Sadie wasn't convinced her sister's marriage would last, though they'd managed quite well for many months. But David's oldest brother chose to disown his doctoring sibling rather than try to understand his desire to help people. Would he disown the brother who returned from the war a hero? Sadie thought it unlikely.

"You shouldn't be here," she told him now, wishing her traitorous heart would calm.

He glanced around the room. "Here, in David's home," he asked, "or here, generally speaking?"

There was a certain bitterness to his words that she'd never heard before. Her protective instincts flared, an odd sensation to a woman who'd never felt protective of a man before and certainly never this one. While she welcomed the disappearance of the desire, she didn't care for this new feeling either.

She pointed at the floor. "Here." *Anywhere near me,* she wanted to add.

"Where else would I go? This is, or was, my home too."

"Not since you left."

Her voice broke on the words. Fearing she'd reveal far more than she was ready to, she pushed past him. He caught her arm as she passed.

"Wait."

She jerked against his hold, keeping her face turned away. "Release me, James, or you'll be sorry."

The words were barely audible. As he leaned closer, refusing to let go, she took a step back. Just when he least expected it, she lunged forward, knocking him back. He fell, hard, but she had no sympathy in her. He'd revived the horror of losing her child, their child, and the pain of loneliness that came with it. She had no time to reassure him, not when her heart was already shattered in her chest.

# Chapter Four

He knew he shouldn't have come. He could have gone anywhere else, but his heart beckoned him to Sadie's side. As she exited the room, he dragged his body upright. The ache in his leg would not be ignored, not after suffering a blow as she'd just delivered. The Miller sisters were no weak females, but hardworking commoners who'd learned long ago to defend their persons from importuning men. There were no ladylike protestations from them, just swift warnings of physical violence and little pause in carrying out the threat. He'd known better, but somehow, in the time he'd been gone, he'd convinced himself she was a lady like any other.

He smiled through the pain, oddly reassured by her unladylike reminder. After all, it was the commoner he'd fallen in love with, not the brainless lady he conjured in his deepest nightmares.

He came upon no one as he made his way to his chamber. His brother employed few servants, money not being plentiful enough to do so. Sadie and her sisters performed most of the duties often put upon servants and they did so without complaint. They were used to a much harder life than the one they currently led, so he was not surprised at their ready acceptance of this one.

James was the one unwilling to accept it. He'd rebelled against the mere thought of having to do for himself, let alone others. His debts and disregard for the consequences of his actions forced him into service in the king's army. His oldest brother applauded the decision, accepting him fully back into the family fold, while David merely nodded and indicated it was for the best, under the circumstances.

And James would have returned, little changed, had it not been for his precious Isabel.

The child was with a lady friend, one he trusted to care for her while he furthered his suit with Sadie. He wasn't certain how she would feel about Isabel and he didn't want the child hurt by a rejection.

James sighed. He'd made a right mess of his life. Falling for a resurrectionist, as his brother had, would effectively remove their oldest brother's good opinion, but James had lived his life quite happily without it. He felt little guilt over disappointing that man yet again.

David, however, was someone James held in high esteem, though he often felt the man was more sanctimonious than the situation called for. Having done such wrong to David's wife and thus to David himself, James was willing to do anything David asked. He'd served his country, a country he barely believed in, and was injured in the line of a duty he barely recognized as his own. But James was not naïve enough to think it was enough to right the wrongs he'd done to.

And it seemed Sadie was of like mind.

His chamber door opened but he didn't turn. "Come to ask me to leave, David?"

There was no response. James glanced over his shoulder, his eyes widening at the identity of his visitor. He turned.

"Mrs. Melbourne," he greeted with a formal bow to his sister-by-marriage. He said nothing more, as he wasn't sure what to say. She looked well, her round form indicating a child would arrive soon, but there was a concerning sadness in her gaze as she looked upon him that he didn't understand.

"James."

Her lack of formality should have reassured him, put him at ease, but it did the opposite. He leaned heavily upon his cane, the ache in his leg growing with each passing moment. He refused to utter the next word. It must be on her to explain her reason for being there, for visiting his chamber in a shocking breach of decorum.

Her sigh was heartfelt. "James, I am pleased you are returned, well and safe,"—her gaze lingered on his cane —"but I must ask you to leave. Return to the baron and partake of his hospitality. He will not turn you away."

"Unlike you and your sister," James couldn't help but point out.

She flinched. "I would not, James, if not for Sadie. She has been through too much and I cannot have you here, a constant reminder of all she has lost and that which she can never have."

His brow furrowed at her words, but he did not address Melly's curious statement. Instead, he focused on the crux of the matter, as he saw it. "What must I do to prove my heart is hers?"

"Your heart was never in question," Melly soothed, "merely your constancy."

"Then what must I do?"

"I know not. Promises are easily broken and you've shown on numerous occasions that honor is not something you can boast." Her words stung, but he said nothing in his defense. Truly, he had none.

"Will leaving again ease the pain it brought her before?"

"This time will be different," Melly said, her dark brows drawing down. She laid a hand on her distended belly. "This time will be different."

Her words were so low he almost missed them. Frowning, he watched the way her fingers clenched over her unborn child, the protective gesture saying far more than it should have. She couldn't be referring to them, as her love for his brother went beyond any paltry feelings she might have entertained towards James. There was only one thing she could mean, only one thing that involved her sister, him, and a difference in his leaving this time.

Horror swept over him. He gave her the only answer he could, the only word that sprang to mind.

"No."

# Chapter Five

James had always considered Society far too strict when it came to their virgins. Forcing a gentleman to marry a lady simply because they happened to be in the same room for a brief moment was ridiculous and unfair. It led to heiresses being compromised for their inheritance and gentlemen inadvertently compromising grasping chits out for a title.

But James had done more than compromise a lady. No, that wasn't quite true. Sadie was no lady and no one would think ill of him for abandoning her to her fate. He'd be condemned for lying with her at all, dregs of humanity that she was. No one would listen to his avowals that she was purer, more true of heart, more honest than any lady he'd ever had the misfortune to meet. Her birth was against her.

He no longer cared, if he ever really did. To him, a pretty maid had ever been a pretty maid and he was never very selective in his choices. His past with Melly proved that. But his youthful transgressions were based in the inane belief that he was entitled to whatever his careless heart desired.

Now he was faced with a woman he loved more than life, a woman he suspected loved him against her better judgment, and he had to convince her that he'd not abandoned her lightly, that he'd not have abandoned her at all had he known.

Another child. Another *dead* child. What a miserable

example of manhood he was!

The house was settling for sleep, though David still tarried in his dissecting chamber and Melly was about her evening duties. James didn't bother creeping through the corridors; the clicking of his cane made that impossible. He strode with halting steps, his goal the small chamber at the end.

He burst in, not bothering to knock. Sadie was not yet abed, retiring at such an early hour not in her nature, but stood by the window, her gaze trained on something without.

She turned as he entered, her eyes widening. "Jamie?"

"You said nothing!" He launched his attack without thought, incensed at himself and at her. "You bore our child and said nothing!"

"You have no right—!" she began, choking back an onslaught of tears that had only just abated. "You left! You hared off on some grand adventure, looking to die on the battlefield and escape responsibility for all the pain you've caused. You—have—no—right!"

Each word brought her closer, anger radiating from every inch of her slim form. "You left me to birth a child, to lose a child, alone!"

"I didn't know!"

The shouted words echoed off the walls, bouncing around them and fading into nothingness. Sadie took a single step back and stared at him, the glow from the fire highlighting the hardness of her expression.

"Would knowing have made a difference?"

"Yes."

The lack of hesitation seemed to startle her. She flinched. "I couldn't know that," she protested.

"And for good reason you chose to believe I'd abandon you to your fate regardless."

They stared at each other. James sighed, defeat and self-loathing consuming him. He could blame her for nothing. Every decision she made was due to his own lack of honor, his own ungentlemanly behavior.

"I am sorry, Sadie, my love," he told her, knowing a simple apology could never be enough.

She shrugged as if it mattered little, but he caught the slight tremble of her shoulders. When she reached up to brush at her cheeks he could be still no longer. He closed the distance between them, drawing her into his embrace. She resisted, but no real strength lay behind the hands she pushed into his chest.

Her sobs soaked his shirt front. An ache settled in his chest at her misery, a misery he caused with his carelessness, his lack of honor. He could not undo it, but he could do everything in his power to prove he'd changed.

If she'd let him.

"I am changed," he whispered.

His words were heartfelt, but the reaction he received called him a liar. Sadie struggled free, an easy thing to do since he immediately released her. He'd not have a repeat of his earlier humiliation at her hands.

"Words, Jamie! More words! There is nothing you can say to prove you've changed." Her sigh shuddered through her, a single tear trickling down her cheek. "And I have nothing left to give."

He gave her the space she seemed to need, taking another step back. He searched her face, searched for some sign that he had a chance with her, a chance to right his wrongs.

He saw nothing to encourage his suit.

"Then I shall leave you. I am needed elsewhere." He sketched a bow and turned on his heel. Tears burned his eyes, but he held them back. He had no one to blame but himself. And tears would do no good.

# Chapter Six

Sadie didn't know what prompted her to do so, but she found herself following James when he took his leave of David and Melly that evening. She followed him through streets she knew intimately, until he came to a small domicile only a few streets away. A woman answered his knock, a beautiful woman whose dress bodice was cut too low and whose skirt was cut too high. A whore.

Sadie's heart hardened. Of course. He made no progress getting beneath her own skirts so he ran to one of his other whores. Her lip curled. It was no more than she deserved for ever lying with him in the first place.

She hugged the wall before her, careful to avoid detection while still able to watch her erstwhile lover and his doxy. He glanced down, smiling brightly. A small hand reached up to tug at his sleeve. As Sadie watched, James reached down and scooped up a beautiful, dark-haired child.

James with a child? Why was Sadie surprised? He'd probably fathered enough bastards to populate the entire East End. Her hand strayed to her empty womb. More fool her for wanting him regardless.

She turned to leave, promising herself there would be no more pining for a man so unworthy of her time. It was silly of her to follow him in the first place.

"Sadie!"

Her eyes slid shut. Now she must explain her reason for

following him. It would be a miracle if he didn't believe her to be a love-smitten fool.

She turned, every movement hesitant, a true testament of her reluctance to face him. But she was Sadie Miller, bastard daughter of a resurrectionist, an outspoken woman of the streets. Surely she could face the author of her misery?

Her spine straightened, almost of its own accord. She'd face him, tell him how she felt about his secret life.

And his whore.

She didn't stop to think that she might be the whore, that for all she knew the woman in the house was his wife, and the girl their daughter. She didn't stop to think anything at all, reacting out of pure emotion, rage, disappointment, and heartbreak.

He reached her and she struck out. But Sadie was Sadie and it wasn't the flat of her hand connecting to his cheek as it would be with most ladies striking out at a gentleman—if ladies even did such a thing. No, Sadie balled up her fist and landed him a facer he'd not soon forget.

Oh, how he'd missed her! James couldn't help but smile, even as he winced. Sadie dabbed at the new cut on his cheekbone, her glowering expression discouraging explanations. She tended to the wound she'd bestowed upon him, just as if it was her right to do so.

He stared at her. She refused to meet his eye, but that didn't stop him from willing her to do just that. As she frowned over his injury, an injury that was nothing, really, she blinked once, hard. It took him a moment to realize what plagued her eyes. Tears threatened to spill down her cheeks. His Sadie never cried, yet she'd done so twice in his presence just since his return.

He reached up and stilled her fingers. "Love, nothing has occurred to warrant your tears."

"Bloody hell, Jamie!" She slapped his hand away. "You can say that? Now? Here?" She gestured around the tiny kitchen they occupied. "We stand in the home of your...your..."

"Friend?" he offered, brows rising, holding back the unwarranted pleasure he felt in her intimate use of his childhood appellation.

She snarled a curse at him that managed to surprise him. Sensing the source of her anger, he took her hand and held tight against her tugs to be free. "Sadie, Catalina is but a friend...now. She cares for Isabel, my ward. Nothing more."

"I don't believe—your ward?"

Ah, that got her attention. "Yes, love, Isabel is my ward. She was orphaned in that god-awful war and I couldn't just leave her there, looting bodies in the middle of a battlefield."

"Looting bodies?"

He seemed to have found the subject that would render her effectively mute, other than an uttered repetition here and there of his own words. "Yes, a little trick she'd learned from her parents who did the same, right up until a soldier they tried to kill decided they'd leave this world before him."

"Is she...unbalanced?"

"Are you?"

Sadie frowned. "A child looting the dead...oh. I see. Of course."

She gave him a long look and James sat silently, hoping something in his actions would prove to her that he'd changed. He didn't have to take the child in and he'd certainly not done it with the intention of using her to win Sadie over. Indeed, he'd fully intended to leave Isabel with David and Melly, freeing him to return to his loveless, empty existence until he ended up dead. It wasn't until he returned to Catalina's and saw the joy on Isabel's face that he'd realized she was his child now, and she was his responsibility, not David's. He would care for her and if she was his only love until the day he died, it was probably for the best.

Now, watching Sadie battle whatever thoughts fought for dominance in her head, he wondered if Isabel might not be the unexpected key to everything he wanted and didn't deserve.

And it didn't matter, he realized. If Sadie wanted him,

she'd have him, sins and all. It wouldn't be a child that changed her mind. She'd come to him on her terms, when she was ready.

He stood as Catalina and Isabel entered the room. "It is time I see that Isabel is in her bed. She would stay up all night if I let her." He smiled to soften the blow of his abandonment, offering a proper bow.

Sadie shook her head, one hand clamping down on his arm to prevent his leaving. "No, you do not escape me that easily, James Arthur Melbourne." He almost flinched at her use of his full name. She shot a glare over her shoulder at Catalina.

James read the look correctly and offered that woman a smile. "Would you be so good as to ready Miss Isabel for bed, Catalina? I will join her presently for her bedtime story." Catalina nodded, her eyes narrowed as she glanced at Sadie. A moment later the woman and her charge disappeared into the back room where Catalina slept.

"You have my attention, Miss Miller."

Sadie released him, wrapping her arms around her middle as if needing the support. "You are a wastrel."

He nodded.

"A rake."

He nodded again, not caring for the line the conversation was taking.

"A scoundrel."

He wasn't quite sure he was that bad, but he'd let her

have her say.

"And a liar."

"Now, wait a moment," he protested, actually insulted. "That is not true."

"Is it not? You had a child with my sister and lied about it. You lied to your brother about her. You tried to end their relationship and very nearly succeeded. You are a miserable excuse of a man and certainly no gentleman."

Oh, she had a point, and James certainly had his faults, but he hadn't lied, not to her and not to David. "I did not know who Melly was, Sadie. I didn't know until she revealed it. That doesn't make me a liar, it makes me a rake. I don't deny that. I never knew about her child, about Olivia, until the moment you discovered Melly's deception. Lying about children seems to be a fault in the Miller women."

Sadie sucked in an outraged breath at his accusation, but James would not be silenced now. He moved one step closer, ignoring the cane propped against the chair. "I admit to many of the faults you've named and more, but to call me a liar is unfair."

Her pale brows lifted, her hands moving to her hips. "Very well. But what of David and Melly? I was there, Jamie, I know what you told him. I can only assume you did so for a reason." She paused, her very silence accusing him of all manner of atrocities. "What was it? Did you envy your brother's future happiness so much you sought to destroy it? Or did you want Melly for yourself?"

He was too shocked to reply right away. "Did I want...? Have you taken leave of your senses?!"

"What was I to think? You protested so vehemently in a marriage that concerned you not at all. You could have kept your secrets, allowing Melly to keep hers."

"It was shame!" he snapped. "Shame at the idea of my family aligning themselves with resurrectionists! Shame at the idea of my brother marrying my castoff!" He growled, snatching up his cane. "Shame at myself for caring one way or the other. It was shame, plain and simple."

He turned to leave. He was done. He'd made mistakes and that was something he had to live with.

He should have made his way to Isabel and the promise of a bedtime story. But his steps led him to the door. He needed air, to escape for just a few moments, clear his head and pray that his careless confession hadn't destroyed any shred of love Sadie might have felt for him.

Just as his hand touched the latch, he paused. "Mostly, Sadie, it was the action of a selfish child who always sought to get his own way. Just as I treated you."

# Chapter Seven

Hell, Sadie couldn't let him leave on that admission. She leapt forward to stop him.

"Papa James?"

The small, heavily-accented voice halted Sadie's advance. She turned to the little girl that she'd yet to formally meet. In her desire to berate James, causing him an injury she felt duty-bound to treat, introductions had fallen to the wayside. At the time, she'd cared little, having no desire to meet James' whore—former whore—as well.

Isabel trotted over to James, her eyes on Sadie. "Papa James?"

"Yes, poppet?" He lifted her in his arms, despite his clear desire to be gone from Sadie's presence.

Isabel launched into a language Sadie didn't know, chattering faster and faster as she sought to make James understand that she was waiting for him.

James responded softly in the same tongue—though his was decidedly less flowing than the child's—earning him a sweet smile and a tender kiss on the cheek. Isabel traipsed back to her bed where Catalina waited with an indulgent smile.

"What was that?"

James frowned. "*That*, as you so charmingly put it, is Isabel."

The steel in his tone surprised her. He was protective of the child, a little girl who didn't share his blood, a girl born of thieves. How his family would rage at the addition of a lowborn foundling.

For the first time in months, since the day James had walked out of her life, Sadie's spirits lifted. She smiled in the face of his anger. "I meant the speech. What language was that?"

James exhaled, his lips twitching as if he, too, wished to smile. "Spanish. Isabel knows no other, though she is learning some English."

"To please her *Papa James*, no doubt."

"Sadie, I have obligations. Isabel has taken me to task for neglecting her while she waited patiently for her story. If there is nothing else you require, I will excuse myself." He waited a moment, adding, "It was good to see you again. Take care."

He'd moved several steps toward the bedchamber before Sadie found her tongue. "Is that all you have to say?"

He didn't turn. "What else is there to say? Nothing."

"You return from war, injured, claiming to have changed. You return with a child, a foundling any other nobleman would have left to die without a second thought."

James' shoulders tensed beneath his form-fitting coat. Sadie waited for him to turn, to speak, anything, but he did none of those things. He walked away from her.

Oh no, he would not run away from her again! "Jamie?" She didn't raise her voice, but she did employ a sultry tone that she knew would catch his attention.

He sighed, turning. "Sadie, no games. Please."

"No games," she assured him. "Only truth. You shared your thoughts with me, now allow me to share mine." She took a steadying breath, her gaze darting to the chamber beyond James. He caught her glance and moved to secure the door separating them from Catalina and Isabel. Though Sadie knew Catalina might still hear some of their speech, she had no choice but to continue.

"You admit to attempting to separate my sister and your brother. I knew that then, and it didn't change my feelings for you. You came home, expecting me to be the same." His brow furrowed at her words, as if he didn't understand what she was saying. Barely understanding herself, she continued.

"I have changed too, Jamie, in ways I don't even understand. I need more than a tumble, more than a rake who casts his glance at anything in a skirt. I'm not sure I can trust you. I am not a well-bred lady who will close her eyes to the truth of her man straying."

James' hand tensed over the head of his cane. His gaze shifted from Sadie to the door behind him, and Sadie's heart sank. Did he still desire Catalina, a woman from his past? Perhaps he longed for Melly, and Sadie was an acceptable replacement. Sadie's heart, the heart she'd thought broken with the loss of her child, broke a little more. He may have changed in some ways, but a rake never changed.

She bobbed a curtsy. "I will leave you to your...*obligations*," she murmured, fighting the sorrow that threatened to bring tears to her eyes again, for the third time that day. What a useless girl she was to cry at every little thing!

"Sadie, will you wait?" James asked. He gestured to the chair he'd vacated earlier. "Please. There is something I must tell you, but I must tend to Isabel first."

Curiosity pushed Sadie down into the chair. She was ready to listen, though believing what he said would be something else entirely.

# Chapter Eight

James pondered what to say to Sadie and how to say it. He kissed Isabel's cheek and settled her under the blanket. Catalina smiled at him from her seat by the window, where the evening's summer light allowed her to mend the garment in her lap.

"You always told the best stories," the woman said, something in her tone making him frown.

He stood, leaning heavily on his cane. Approaching the other woman, he stated, "You think me a liar, as well."

Catalina cocked her head. "No, not a liar. Not in your mind. You tell things the way you hear them, the way you understand them. Not a liar. *Engañado*."

"Ah. Misled. That isn't really different, though, is it?"

She shrugged, as if it mattered little. "Love can overlook much in a man. Perhaps your woman, who can forgive so much in you, can overlook this." She then shifted away from him, indicating she'd had her say and would input no more.

James left her. His association with Catalina was over many years ago, before he'd met Melly for the second time. He'd thought little of her since, but when Isabel came into his life, he'd remembered the Spanish woman and decided she would be a good person to bring Isabel to should David and Melly be unwilling to take the child.

Sadie remained in the other room, the kitchen/sitting room that served Catalina very well. James moved to stand before her, oddly surprised at the sense of peace he felt. Normally, he would run, or want to run. Not anymore. Whether Sadie accepted him or not, James would remain in London, close to his brother, raising his adopted daughter.

"Would you like to know the truth, Sadie?"

She nodded up at him, saying nothing.

"Very well." James grasped another chair and swung it around to face Sadie's. He lowered himself carefully. His leg protested. He'd been on his feet too much that day and Sadie's multiple assaults on his person caused more discomfort than he cared to admit.

He stretched his leg out, wincing as he did so. Fire shot through the limb. He couldn't suppress the gasp of pain.

Sadie leaned forward, laying her hands on his aching leg. He nearly came off the chair at the contact.

"Be at ease," she murmured, a smile playing about her lips. Her fingers worked gently, massaging the soreness down to a manageable state. "I am sorry for furthering your injury," Sadie whispered, not meeting his eyes.

"As am I," he responded. "I feel my return has caused you more pain than my abandonment."

She shrugged. "Perhaps. Let us leave it at that. We are each of us sorry creatures."

Silence fell. The sensations coursing through James' leg held less fire with each passing moment, but the fire was replaced with a headier sensation, far more base and primitive. He turned his thoughts inward, trying to resist the urge to still Sadie's hands, pull her into his lap and remind her just how well they got on together.

Blessed relief, Sadie removed her hands of her own volition. Desire still hummed through James, but he could manage it, as he had since he'd left her side many months before.

Then he looked in her eyes. Devil take it, she stared at him with as much hunger as he felt, yet he knew what would happen if they gave in to their desires. Things must be said, and he'd be damned if he let something happen that would lead her to hate him more. He'd not be accused of seducing her into submission!

"Sadie, my love, I have not been with a woman since you."

His statement sent the expected shock through his love. Her eyes widened and her lips moved as if the words she wanted to speak would not come.

"Months, Jamie," she finally said. Her gaze slid over him, lingering on places of his anatomy that caused the heat to rise.

"And many more before I met you," he further revealed.

It was in opposition of his reputation, and something he'd not even told his brother, but his days of tumbling anything in a skirt had ended long ago. Little of his rakish reputation held true anymore, especially since his gambling was something he'd left behind when he'd left England. His eldest brother had paid the last of his debts and sent him on his merry way, to kill or be killed in battle. James could hardly blame him for that.

He leaned back in his chair and forced his eyes away from Sadie's. It was a small effort in restoring his equilibrium, but desperation called for it. Smoothing a non-existent wrinkle from his pantaloons, he asked, "Does David ever speak to you of his work?"

"Never. I made it quite clear from the start that I wanted to learn nothing of the bodies he dissects or what he discovers when he does so. I was content to assist Melly in the running of the household."

James smiled, chancing a look at her again. Her desire had faded, leaving a mere glimmer in her expression. "Ah, wise girl. Now, me, I stood by his side one day, mere months after I'd met your sister for a second time, and watched him dissect a girl little older than the daughter I never knew I had. She'd died trying to rid herself of a child. David made me watch as he taught me and a few of his students what happens when a desperate girl ingests something vile in order to hide what had happened to her."

He paused, remembering the horror of the time, and the realization that he could have forced any number of women into just such a position. Though forced may have been too strong a word, he knew damn well many women needed money to survive and an extra mouth to feed wasn't something they could take. He'd carelessly assumed that any female of the streets would be well-versed in preventative measures and in his immense arrogance assumed Melly was one of those women. He had no idea he'd seduced an innocent, paying her as if whoring was her life.

"You do not seem to mind the dissection room now."

"I grew used to it, though I spent little time with David after that," he admitted. "One grows used to the horror, after a time."

"I know how that is. I cannot say I was pleased when my father informed me I would help him gather bodies for the anatomy schools."

James held his cane in one hand, his fingers clenching over the knob. "Sadie, all of that has little to do with why we sit here, in Catalina's home, while darkness falls around us."

At his words, Sadie jumped up. "I'll find candles." She scurried about before he could stop her, poking her fingers into every cupboard she could find until she had a few candles which she lit from the embers in the cooking stove.

But Sadie didn't return to her chair. She paced instead, her body casting odd shadows as she moved before the candles to the window, past the cooking stove and back. James watched her, wondering just what plagued her mind now. Did she believe him, or was it some deeper thought that she battled?

"What am I to do?" she finally snapped, casting a glance towards the other chamber and then lowering her voice. "If

I believe you, if I allow you back into my life, I take a chance that you will break my heart again."

He slowly stood, taking care to lean on his cane to avoid further pain. "And if you don't?"

Her sigh went deep, shaking her slim form. "Then my heart breaks again regardless."

James held back the smile he wanted to release. Victory was at hand and he wanted to crow in triumph. But he held back. Sadie was hurting, expecting him to behave in the same way he had for years. "You love me." She nodded, reluctantly. "But you do not trust me."

"How can I? I have only your word that what you speak is truth."

"You are correct, Miss Miller." He stepped closer, taking her hand. "Have you considered, though, that I have only your word as well? How am I to know I'd not be made a cuckold within a year of our marriage?"

Outrage flared in her expression. "I would never—!"

He leaned down, putting his face eye level with hers. "But how can I know that? Women of your station are not known for their constancy."

Her mouth fell open. "What a disgusting thing to say!"

"Sadie, listen to yourself. We both come from classes that have no concept of fidelity. Is it not fair to say that I take as great a chance on you as you do on me?"

"Fair?" She fell silent, clearly pondering his words.

"Sadie, I promise you, I know my sins. I've made stupid

choices, careless, thoughtless decisions. I've hurt people, my family, your family. My arrogance and selfishness cannot be denied. I fight that in myself now. I have known no woman since you. My every thought in that interminable battle was for you, returning to you, proving my love for you."

"And there was Isabel."

James smiled. "Yes, there was Isabel." The smile faded. "I'd have loved our child, Sadie, our son. I hope you believe that."

She crumpled into his arms. The unexpected movement threw him off balance and he struggled to catch her and maintain his position. He maneuvered her to the chair behind him, settling her there and kneeling before her on his good knee.

"More tears? I begin to think it best to withdraw my suit. My words, my actions bring you nothing but pain."

She lifted her head. The candles revealed twin streaks marring the perfection of her cheeks. "And your leaving will cause more." She wiped at her eyes. Her defeated sigh was belied by the smile curving her lips. "I am a miserable creature without you, Jamie."

"Can I take that to mean you accept me, flaws and all?"

Her smile widened. "Only if you can accept me, flaws and all."

James drew her forward, bringing them both to their feet. His teasing grin enveloped her, drawing forth an answering smile. "Flaws just make life more interesting, love."

His lips met hers in a deep kiss, one of longing and love, the passion of before a smoldering ember in their embrace. Sadie accepted his offering and gave back all the love she felt in her heart, the love she'd held ruthlessly in check. The pain she carried for her lost child and her love intertwined, beginning to heal the crack in her heart. Though she would forever mourn her baby's death, she could rejoice in knowledge that there would be more and James was finally a man she could love without reservation.

# The End

# Additional Author's Note

In this story I have presented the reader with a doctor who runs a very small school of anatomy. This is a figment of my imagination. Though there were a few schools of anatomy at the time, the one I've portrayed is much smaller than what actually existed.

I have also taken certain liberties with the history of resurrectionists to make this story work. There is no record of female body-snatchers. There were a few infamous men who stole bodies for the schools, one of whom I mention in this story, Ben Crouch. Some really did murder people in order to sell the bodies—unfortunately, I didn't make that up.

I've also implied the doctor in this story uses several bodies in his teaching. This is a complete fabrication, even beyond the fact that he and his school never existed. The biggest schools of anatomy only used a few cadavers per year in their teaching, though if they were willing to pay the resurrectionists for illegal bodies, they had more.

The part about stripping the bodies before taking them is true. It was illegal to steal anything from a grave...except the body itself.

# About the Author

Jaimey Grant, a pseudonym for Laura Miller, was born in Michigan in 1979. After a fun-filled childhood interlaced with moments of emotional trauma and an insatiable curiosity about the reasons people act the way they do, she became a writer.

Primarily a Regency romance author, Jaimey has also dabbled in fantasy of a non-romance variety. A comprehensive list of works and where to find them can be found on her website, www.jaimeygrant.com. There are more Regencies and fantasies in the works.

She currently lives in Michigan with her husband and two children.

To learn more about Jaimey and her work, visit any of the sites below.

Website: http://www.jaimeygrant.com
Blog: http://jaimeygrant.blogspot.com

Facebook: http://www.facebook.com/jaimeygrantauthor
Email: jaimeygrant@yahoo.com